HOPJOY
WAS
HERE

A FLAXBOROUGH MYSTERY

Colin Watson

This edition published in 2018 by Farrago, an imprint
of Prelude Books Ltd
13 Carrington Road, Richmond, TW10 5AA, United Kingdom

www.farragobooks.com

By arrangement with the Beneficiaries of the
Literary Estate of Colin Watson

First published by Eyre and Spottiswoode in 1962

ISBN: 978-1-78842-018-1

Have you read them all?

Treat yourself again to the first Flaxborough novels –

Coffin, Scarcely Used
In the respectable town of Flaxborough, an equally respectable councillor is laid to rest. Cause of death: pneumonia . . .

Bump in the Night
It begins with a drinking fountain being blown to smithereens – next the statue of a local worthy loses his head.

Hopjoy Was Here
Two men have disappeared, and something very disagreeable seems to be lurking in the drains.

Turn to the end of this book for a full list of the series, plus – on the last page – the chance to receive **further background material.**

Chapter One

NEVER BEFORE HAD the inhabitants of Beatrice Avenue seen a bath carefully manoeuvred through one of their front doors, carried down the path by four policemen, and hoisted into a black van. Everybody watched, of course; whether from the vantage point of a bedroom window or delicately through parlour lace or with bold and naked curiosity at the gate. A postman was frozen in sidelong contemplation on a doorstep five houses farther up. A butcher's boy and two window cleaners huddled in temporary comradeship with a rate collector on the opposite kerb and stretched involuntarily in time with the policemen's efforts as the bath was lifted and eased along the floor of the van. Twenty or more children, mysteriously summoned by their extra-sensory perception of odd goings-on, formed the nearest and most importunate section of the audience. They savoured the affair with the discrimination of experts, comparing it with the fire in Harley Close two months back, last summer's impaling of the greengrocer's horse, and the wonderful, blood-chilling entertainment in Gordon Road the previous Easter when Mrs Jackson had gone bonkers and thrown all the portable contents of the house, including a gramophone and two chamber pots, down upon some men from the council.

The children jostled for glimpses of the bath, gleaming dimly in the depths of the van. 'Mister, wotcher been and took it out for?' 'Where yer goin' with it, mister?' And a rash jest, thrown out by a bobbing, streaky-faced girl of twelve: 'They're going to wash their socks! All the coppers is going to wash their socks!' There was a quick squawking cadenza of laughter. A little hysteria was mixed in it: not all the children were insensitive to the sinister obscenity of the bath's removal.

Two of the policemen, ponderous and flushed, shut the van's rear doors. Not looking at the children, they paced slowly to the cab and climbed in. As the van drew away, the third policeman made awkward shooing gestures and announced: 'Nothing more to see. Run along home, all of you.' Then he turned with his companion and they went up the little path and into the house, closing the door behind them.

The watchers in Beatrice Avenue remained alert for varying periods but by the end of half an hour only two or three of the chronically curious had not tired of peering at the unrewarding façade of number fourteen and at the black police car that still stood a few yards from its front gate.

Luckier were the occupants of the house in Pawson's Lane that backed on to fourteen Beatrice Avenue. They, a mother and her middle-aged daughter, had a view denied to those who lingered on doorsteps or behind parlour windows.

Overlooking the passageway at the side of number fourteen – a space hidden from the front street by a tall, solid gate – they were able to see the intriguing activities of two men in plain clothes.

This pair worked with a sort of fastidious dedication. They were unhurried and seemed to be taking good care of their suits as they knelt on sheets of newspaper and passed implements to each other like brother surgeons.

Together they levered up the grilled cover plate of a drain, examined it and set it aside. Then, using a long-handled dipper, one began to ladle liquid from the drain and pour it gently through a funnel held by the other into the first of two big Winchesters. At the end of about twenty minutes both bottles were full. The man who had been holding the funnel stoppered them and moved them out of the way.

He next selected and handed to his companion what appeared to be a tea-strainer on the end of a rod and prepared a wide-mouthed glass jar to receive whatever might be dredged.

The strainer was lowered into the drain. Its manipulator held it lightly and probed for a few seconds like a well-bred guest trying to determine whether his hostess had sugared his tea. When the strainer was withdrawn its mesh held a black, dripping slime-bound miscellany. This was allowed to drain awhile, then turned and tapped out into the jar.

A second and a third exploration produced further gobbets of solid but as yet unidentifiable matter. Patiently as anglers, the kneeling pair went on with their task until the strainer repeatedly emerged empty. Then one replaced the drain grill, the other screwed down the lid of the jar, and both stood, stretching gratefully and plucking straight their trouser creases.

The old woman, perched on the side of her bed, her chin resting on arms folded on the window sill, acknowledged with a grunt the completion of the operation. But she did not take her eyes from the opposite passageway.

Her daughter, a desiccated woman with a cruel, helmet-like perm, and an air of irreparable disappointment, did not move either. She continued to stand stiffly at her mother's side, holding the curtain like a shield in apprehension of a flight of arrows.

'What have they found, Mirrie?' the old woman whispered.

'I don't know. Something in the drains. I can't see any more than you.'

'Do you think Mr Periam knows they're there? The police, I mean. It is the police, Mirrie. That one in the grey who's just gone in – I saw him at the station when I went about the purse. It's funny Mr Periam's not there, though.'

'He's still away, I expect.'

'What about the other chap, his friend or lodger or whoever he was?'

'I don't know about him.'

There was a pause. 'It's funny about all those policemen,' the old woman said. 'Policemen don't clear drains.' She sounded annoyed rather than intrigued.

The daughter said nothing. She moved the curtain a little farther aside and watched a short ladder being placed carefully against the wall by the remaining occupant of the passageway – the one not in grey. He climbed and peered into the cup of the fall pipe. After exploring delicately with one finger and apparently finding nothing of interest, he descended, laid the ladder down beside the dividing fence, and entered the house.

This now contained two uniformed constables, who had put their helmets side by side on a table in the kitchen and were standing, large, uneasy and tousle-browed near the front door; the plain-clothed pair who had been busy outside; a plumber strapping up his bag in the denuded, forlorn-looking bathroom; and two sharply contrasted but seemingly intimate figures who systematically searched and appraised the stuffy, brown, shiny-papered dining-room.

One of these was several inches over six feet tall; he stood loosely, as if good-humouredly apologetic for his bulk, and looked around with his head slightly on one side like a very high class auctioneer deliberately ignoring the bids of merely moneyed men. He had the firm, amused mouth of a good listener. Now and then he ran long fingers through springy, corn-coloured hair.

His companion was shorter by a head, but made of a lot of prime meat. His smooth, glowingly healthy face looked about eleven years old. It had set like that, in point of fact, twenty-three years before, when he really was eleven.

The man with yellow hair opened the doors of a mahogany sideboard and knelt to look inside. On one shelf there were neatly stacked piles of patterned china and some folded table linen. The second shelf contained some bags of sugar, cruet and butter dish, three opened packets of various breakfast cereals, jars of jam and marmalade, a supply of canned food, and a basin with about an inch of a white, congealed substance in the bottom. It had set around the bristles of a broad paint brush.

'Excuse me....'

A third man had silently entered the room. He looked inquiringly at each of the searchers. 'Detective Inspector Purbright?'

The kneeling man rose. 'I'm Purbright.'

'Good-O!' The new arrival grinned and launched himself at the inspector with a curious crouching stride, his hand extended like that of a Japanese wrestler. After involuntarily stepping back a pace, Purbright braced himself and allowed his arm to be pumped.

'My name's Warlock. Hang-'em-on-a-thread Department.' He peered kindly into Purbright's face and added: 'Forensic science lab, you know. I understand I might be able to help you, squire.'

Purbright murmured politely, introduced his companion as Detective Sergeant Love, and gave Mr Warlock a quick but careful scrutiny.

The man seemed to be itching to play basketball. He kept stretching up on his toes, flexing first one leg then the other, and swaying gently from side to side. Every now and then he touched finger-ends and drew them apart again with delicate restlessness.

Love regarded him sullenly. He put him down as a cluehog, an alien live wire.

Still undulating like an undersea plant at the turn of the tide, Warlock glanced rapidly round the room. 'What's supposed to have been going on?' he asked. 'I've only just got here. They didn't tell me much.'

'I'm not surprised. We're in a bit of a vacuum at the moment, Mr Warlock.' Purbright drew out two of the cold seated, rigidly matched dining chairs. 'Here, we'd better sit down for a minute.'

Warlock abandoned his limbering up exercises and perched in an attitude of comparatively immobile attention. The sergeant turned his back and started going through the contents of a varnished oak bureau surmounted by twin cupboards behind leaded glass: an arrangement that Love approvingly voted 'dinky'.

'The day before yesterday,' Purbright began, 'we received an anonymous letter. That was ... yes, Tuesday. I haven't got it with me at the moment but I can give you the gist of it. "Why don't you take a look into fourteen Beatrice Avenue because I'm sure something awful has happened there." That was the first sentence, I remember. Then there came some rather confused stuff about a lot of noise coming from the house last Thursday night and what did we make of that? You'll have noticed how damnably rhetorical these anonymous letter writers always are?'

Warlock nodded his small, very round head. His face, Purbright reflected, was that of a vigorous, self-employed artisan: weathered, a little coarse, but perkily good-humoured. He had thick, straight hair, carefully combed low across the forehead, and as he nodded a hank of it slipped down to the bridge of his button nose; he reached automatically for the comb in the breast pocket of his rumpled sports jacket.

'The letter posed a few more questions, all very portentous. Why should someone want to dig in the garden at two in the morning? Why was the bathroom light on half the night? That sort of thing.'

Purbright stared past Warlock through the glass panelled door that led to a small formal garden. 'We don't take much notice of our back bedroom vigilantes as a rule. They're mostly old friends, of course, and we'd rather they worked their persecution mania off on us instead of mangling the neighbours. This letter was different, though. For one thing, it didn't hint at fornication. Secondly, it was just a bit more circumstantial than usual. And thirdly ...'

Purbright's voice trailed off. He watched a big grey cat, gloomily hunch-shouldered, picking its way along the fence at the bottom of the garden.

Warlock glanced behind him just as the cat halted, turned its head at right angles and scowled. 'Thirdly?' prompted Warlock. The cat presented its rear, its tail momentarily a quivering exclamation mark, and disappeared into the farther garden.

'Well, as a matter of fact we did happen to know a little about the set-up here,' Purbright was speaking more carefully. 'Nothing sinister, but there were features that might be thought unusual.'

Again he paused. Then, 'Look I know you'll think this damned stupid and starchy, but can I have a peek at your identification?'

Warlock stared, grinned, disinterred a slim wallet from a bunch of papers and handed it to the inspector. Purbright glanced at it apologetically and hastily returned it. 'I do hope you didn't mind.'

'Not a bit of it, squire. Who did you think I was, anyway – Philby?'

Purbright shrugged. 'Everyone goes through the prescribed motions nowadays. The discipline of disbelief. It's supposed to make us feel safe.'

The chained onyx light-bowl in the centre of the ceiling rattled as footsteps passed across the floor of the room above. Purbright leaned towards Sergeant Love.

'Sid, I think you'd better clear those lads outside again. Tell them to get a spade apiece and do some gardening. The places to try will be obvious enough still – if there are any, of course.'

Love moved to the door.

'Oh, and there's no need for both the uniformed men to stay. Peters can go back to the station.' Purbright turned to Warlock again. 'You'll not want a herd of them trampling on your insufflator. Now let's get on with the story.

'There are – or were – two people living in this house. Both fellows in their late thirties. Not related. The actual householder is called Gordon Periam. He keeps a tobacconist's shop in the town. The house he inherited from his mother. She was a widow and they lived here together until her death just over a year ago.

'The name of the other chap is Brian Hopjoy. He's supposed to be a commercial traveller based here in Flaxborough with a line in pharmaceutical sundries, or something like that. Is there such a thing?'

'I believe so,' Warlock said.

'Aye, well it doesn't matter much; I gather the travelling job is just a cover for something else. Anyway, Hopjoy turned up a few months before the old woman died and she took him in as a lodger.'

Warlock fleetingly reviewed the solid, carefully tended furniture. 'Paying guest, surely,' he amended.

'Quite. It seems to have been a pretty amicable arrangement because after Mrs Periam's death Hopjoy stayed on. I don't know how they managed for meals and cleaning up; there's no sign of a regular housekeeper, although the woman next door says a girl came round occasionally. She thinks she was a friend. We'll sort that out in time.'

Purbright saw that Warlock had had enough of sitting. Refusing a cigarette, he began to rock slowly on the very edge of his chair and to make short chopping gestures with his hands. The inspector looked away. 'I wonder if you can see an ashtray anywhere ...'

Gratefully Warlock leapt to his feet and began a spring-heeled, neck-craning tour of the late Mrs Periam's ornaments.

Purbright flicked his ash into the fireplace and resumed his story.

'I wasn't at the station when that letter arrived on Tuesday. The sergeant was rather sceptical – naturally enough, on the face of it – and he just sent one of the uniformed men round to ring the bell and give the place the once over. There was no one in, and they left it at that.

'Yesterday morning the letter was reported to me. I took it straight to the Chief Constable – have you met old Chubb, by the way?' Warlock, peering at a row of silver trophies on the sideboard, shook his head. 'Oh, you must,' said Purbright. 'He thinks that crimes in this town are committed only in his policemen's imagination. This time he's worried, though.'

'It doesn't look as if he need be on Periam's account,' Warlock said. He had finished reading the inscriptions on the cups. 'Athletic type.'

'So was Samson.' Purbright looked at his watch. 'No, the position is this, Mr Warlock. Both these characters are missing. There may be a perfectly innocent explanation – despite the anonymous letter – but we don't think so. One of the pair happens to be in a rather special category. Only the Chief and I know about that and I'm afraid we'll have to keep it to ourselves for the moment, but I can assure you that it makes an important difference. At least – I'm supposed to think so.'

'You don't sound too certain.'

Purbright smiled. 'That's just my parochialism; we like to think our crimes are home grown.'

'Even murders?'

'Murders especially.'

'And in this case ...'

'In this case. Mr Warlock, I must beg you not to try and relieve me of confidences, however much I deplore having them thrust upon me. The fact of murder has yet to be established. That is why you are here.'

'Leave it to me, squire. Any pointers?' Again Warlock was the eager handyman.

'There are one or two things we've noticed. I'll show them to you now.'

As the two men were about to leave the room, Sergeant Love's shining face appeared in the doorway. 'They've started, sir. There was a spade in the garage.' He glanced over at the garden door and added approvingly: 'This rain's just come at the right time to soften things up a bit for them.'

'It's as well, then,' Purbright said to Warlock, 'that I had that drain emptied. A heavy shower would have flushed it.' He stepped into the narrow, carpeted passage and walked to the foot of the stairs near the front door.

'Drain?'

'Yes. It's all nicely bottled for you. The stuff from the bathroom, you know.'

'Bathwater, do you mean?'

Purbright winced. 'Good Lord, no. I mean Mr Periam – or Mr Hopjoy. In solution.'

Chapter Two

WARLOCK SURVEYED THE bathroom with the tense incredulity of a curator viewing empty picture frames after a burglary.

'I'm sorry if we've been a bit impetuous,' said Purbright, just behind him. 'The Chief Constable was anxious to have the prize exhibit kept somewhere safe. It's over at our place; you can see it whenever you like.'

'Yes, but prints ...'

'Oh, don't worry, we collected what there were of those before the plumber was set loose. In any case, he was told to touch nothing but the pipes.'

Warlock looked far from reassured but he stepped forward into the centre of the floor to make room for the inspector to stand beside him.

Purbright pointed to the wall opposite the dusty, water-stained rectangle from which the bath had been taken. It bore a number of tiny splashes, dark brown against the green distemper which ran from the white half-tiling to the ceiling. The group of marks was at Warlock's head level. He gave it close, rapidly ranging scrutiny, like a short-sighted man reading a telegram, then briskly he turned to Purbright. 'And the next, squire?'

'Down here ... and here ...' With his foot Purbright indicated two points at which the grey linoleum was just perceptibly stained. Immediately, Warlock was down on his knees. 'Could be,' he said. 'There's been some wiping up, though.'

By what seemed effortless levitation Warlock stood up and looked expectantly at Purbright once more.

Purbright resisted the temptation to confess aloud that he was beginning to feel like the feed man in some bizarre variety turn. Quietly he went to the small mirror-fronted cabinet above the wash-basin and opened its door. 'We found this tucked away in the corner under the bath. It's all right; nobody's handled it.'

Warlock leaned over the wash-basin and stared at the hammer lying on a sheet of stiff card in the lower compartment of the cabinet. It was an ordinary household hammer, weighing perhaps a little over a pound. He withdrew it carefully, using the cardboard as a tray.

In the light from the window the fore part of the hammer head looked brownly varnished. A few hairs clung to it.

Warlock drew in his lips and released them with a popping noise. 'So much for the do-it-yourself kit' – he replaced the hammer in the cabinet – 'but what about the job it was used for?' He glanced again at the wall splashes and turned to Purbright.

'I'm afraid that's not going to be so easy to answer just at the moment. Come here a minute.'

The inspector stepped to the space where the bath had stood. He bent down and pointed to a black circle, about half an inch across. Joining him, Warlock saw that the mark was actually a shallow depression, charred but sticky. The linoleum and part of the board beneath had been burned away.

'He was carefully tidy. That's the only drop he spilled.' Purbright rubbed his chin gloomily. 'I wonder what he felt like when he pulled the plug and heard his pal going down the pipe with that awful ghwelphing noise.'

Undaunted by this speculation, Warlock touched the blackened indentation daintily with his little finger, which he then sniffed at and promptly rinsed under the wash-basin tap.

'Sulphuric, I imagine,' said Warlock, connoisseur-like. 'He'd have needed a fairish drop. Have you any hopes of tracing where he got it from?'

'We can but try. It seems rather much to hope that he collected it pint by pint from a local chemist's, though. How would one go about laying in, what – several gallons? – of concentrated sulphuric acid? It's not a problem I'm familiar with.'

'The commercial stuff's what you'd want,' Warlock explained. 'There's tons of it going out every day to manufacturers, processing plants, garages, that sort of thing. Industrial chemists are the people: they'd fix you up.'

'But surely they don't run a home delivery service, like paraffin or soft drinks.'

Warlock made one of his impatient, energetic arm gestures. 'What did you say this fellow did for a living – Perry, was it?'

'Periam. He's a tobacconist.'

'No, the other one, then.'

'Hopjoy?'

'The traveller, yes. What was it you said his line was?'

'Pharmaceuticals …' Purbright nodded thoughtfully. 'I see what you mean.' With something less than enthusiasm, he added: 'We'll go into that, of course.'

Warlock sensed that he had wandered again a little too close to some preserve of which the inspector had been appointed an unwilling custodian. The man Hopjoy, it was clear, had a special and secret status. A by-blow of royalty? A relative of the Chief Constable? Warlock was not seriously bothered. Outside the world of fingerprints and fibre strands, which absorbed his considerable dynamism, he was incurious.

He switched back to his own field. 'You've seen the bath?'

'I have, yes.'

'So must I. There would have been problems. I'll be interested to find out how he managed them.'

'Because of the acid, you mean.'

'Certainly. It takes some withstanding. Heavy enamel might do it, but there'd need to be no scratches or chips. A rubber plug would serve. What about the plug seating, though? That's always metal; it would go in no time. Chain, too …' Warlock enumerated the snags zestfully, like a surgeon counting tumours.

'All that,' Purbright interrupted, 'was taken care of. I'll show you when we go downstairs. Is there anything else you want to see here?'

Warlock gave a final deprecatory glance at the twisted, sealed-off plumbing, peered briefly into an empty airing cupboard, then went again to the cabinet. He looked at the jars and packets on the single shelf above the hammer.

They included one of the less inhibited after-shave lotions, a box labelled 'Friar Martin's Herbal Blood-purifying Lozenges', a lidless tin of rather dusty first-aid dressings, a jar of Riding Master Hand Salve (Cherrywood), and another of anti-scurf ointment, two boxes of laxative pills and a plastic dispenser of Man-about-Town Body Acid Neutralizer (Apple Loft).

'An essay in divergent personalities,' murmured the inspector over Warlock's shoulder.

Warlock gingerly shifted one or two of the jars aside. He craned to see the back of the shelf. 'No sign of shaving kit. Did those boys have beards?'

'There's an electric razor in the bureau thing downstairs. I imagine that would go with Riding Master and Man-about-Town. The herbal lozenge addict would be a soaper and scraper.'

'In that case I'd say he was the survivor, then. Took his stuff with him. Hello ...'

Warlock reached into the cabinet with a pair of tweezers and withdrew from among the dressings a small rectangle of metal. It was a single-edged razor blade. 'What's he been doing with this, I wonder.'

He pointed to where the brightness of the steel had been dulled across one corner by a brown deposit.

'Odd,' said Purbright, feeling somewhat lightly armed in the matter of forensic speculation. Warlock carefully propped the razor blade against the hammer shaft. Then he turned and motioned the inspector to lead the way downstairs.

A few steps from the bottom Purbright paused, eyeing the looming obstruction of Constable Donaldson who stood by the front door and darkened the diminutive hallway. 'Bring a chair out and sit down,' Purbright said. 'You make the place look like Downing Street.'

Re-entering the dining-room, they found Sergeant Love had cleared the contents of the bureau out upon the table and was now glancing through the pile of papers he had collected from the drawers and pigeon-holes. Through the half-open window came the sound of an exploratory spade being thrust at fairly long intervals into the dusty soil of the flower beds. The threatened shower had held off. Both men in the garden had removed their jackets. One absent-mindedly swung the trowel he was holding – he had succeeded in being unable to find a spade – and gazed at the earth his colleague had disturbed.

Purbright opened the door of the sideboard and pointed out to Warlock the basin and paint brush.

'I was just looking at this when you arrived. I think it's the answer to some of the questions you were asking upstairs.'

Warlock squatted and examined the basin closely, not touching it. He lowered his head farther and sniffed.

'Wax, isn't it?' Purbright asked.

'Paraffin wax. Melted candles, probably; there's a piece of wick in it.' Warlock rocked gently on his heels and looked up. There was simple pleasure on his face. 'Brushed hot over the plug seating and any breaks in the enamel – just the job, squire. And the chain – that could have been dipped through it.'

Love scowled at the papers that he was now sorting into three heaps which he mentally classified as letters, bills, and odds-and-ends. His resentment of the cheerful Warlock was sharpened by the laboratory man's anticipation of the very theory he had been nurturing in his own mind with the intention of producing it, like a prize marrow, at the opportune moment. He salvaged what credit he could by breaking into the conversation with an announcement.

'That's quite likely to be right, about the bath, inspector. I noticed when I was going over it for prints that there were traces of grease on the bottom.'

'Ah,' said Purbright, nodding sagaciously at Warlock.

'It looked,' added Love, 'rather as if an attempt had been made to rinse it clean with hot water. But whoever did that forgot about the plug chain. It was slung over one of the taps and still quite thickly covered.'

He returned to his sorting.

Warlock regarded the basin with possessive joy. 'One decent dab on you, sweetheart, and ...' – he made the cork-drawing sound that seemed, for him, to symbolise the ultimate in desirable achievement. Love winced.

'It would be very helpful,' Purbright conceded. 'Provided, of course, that we can establish whose print it is. I suppose the presumption must be strong that it belongs to whichever of the two gentlemen is still alive.'

'Bound to, squire.' Warlock glanced round at the inspector as if in wonderment that a man could view a certainty with such caution. 'Mind you,' he added, 'I'm not promising that anything will show up. It's the sort of job for which anyone with sense would wear rubber gloves. Sloshing acid about, and so on. Don't you think so?'

Purbright let the point pass. It seemed unfruitful. 'The hairs on that hammer, now,' he went on. 'How far are they going to be helpful?'

'That's hard to say.' Warlock rose and slipped his restless hands into his trouser pockets, where they continued to rummage like inquisitive mice. 'It's identification you're after again, I suppose. Yes, well, in itself a hair doesn't tell a great deal. It's comparative tests that are significant. Give me hair A and hair B and I'll tell you if they're from the same head – with a reasonable degree of certainty, anyway.'

The inspector considered this offer. Then he addressed Love. 'Sid, I want you to chase some hairs for this gentleman. We'll need to have a pretty fair idea of whom they belong to, though. Periam's shop is one possibility: he may have kept a jacket or something there. We don't know that the other fellow – Hopjoy – had a place of his own, an office or anything. See if there's marked clothing of his among the stuff here.'

'What about initialled hairbrushes, sir?' Love was young in heart.

'Oh yes, rather. Initialled hairbrushes by all means.'

There was a gentle knock on the door and one of the plain-clothes men thrust his head round. 'Excuse me, sir, but we've turned something up.'

'Have you, Mr Boggan?' Purbright sounded pleased.

'Yes, sir. I thought perhaps you'd like to have a look.'

Purbright and Warlock followed him into the garden. It was a neat, uninspiring arrangement of lawn bordered on three sides with flower bed and enclosed by a shoulder-high fence of creosoted boarding. The grass was not rank, but it obviously had not been mown for several weeks. The few plants regularly spaced along the surrounding strip of soil looked like old hotel residents: deep-rooted, uncompromising and reluctant to bloom. A sterile plum tree stood primly in the far corner, its trunk collared with a blackened remnant of clothes line.

Detective Boggan's colleague was on one knee at the edge of the lawn, near a shallow pit in the flower bed. He was brushing soil from a sack that now lay on the grass. Suddenly he snatched away his hand, swore, examined a finger and pressed it to his handkerchief. When he withdrew it there was a glint of scarlet.

'You'd better go in and wash it,' Purbright said. He leaned over the sack. From a small rent protruded a fin of pale green glass. There were several other tiny holes in the sack. They looked like burns.

Purbright gingerly pulled back the neck of the sack. It was full of broken glass, some pieces as much as six or seven inches long. All were slightly concave as if they had formed a huge bottle.

'There's your carboy,' said Warlock. He looked a little longer at the spilling fragments. 'I wonder where he put the basket.'

'Basket?'

'Yes, these acid containers are usually set in iron lattice things like big fire baskets. They're to protect them while they're being shifted about.'

'Buried too, I suppose,' said Purbright. Boggan looked without favour at the stretch of flower bed that remained to be explored.

The detective who had cut his hand came out of the house and walked up to the group on the lawn. 'I think,' he said to the inspector, 'that I know where that thing was smashed up.'

He led Purbright and Warlock back into the kitchen and through a side door that opened into the garage. He pointed to a corner of the floor. 'There's a whole lot of little splinters round there, sir. I noticed them earlier on when I was looking for a spade.'

The others examined the floor, nodded acknowledgement of their guide's perspicacity, and turned their attention to the rest of the garage.

Along one wall, lit now by the sun rays that filtered through a long, grimy skylight, there hung from hooks and nails a rusted saw, an oil-stained pictorial calendar for 1956, a cylinder head gasket, a tyre worn to the canvas, an old scouting haversack and something discernible as porcelain under its covering of dust. Purbright identified it, with some surprise, as a bed pan.

Tools, most of which looked long disused, lay neatly on a workbench supported by brackets at the end of the garage. There were several tins of oil and polish and paint on the shelf above the bench; among the miscellany stacked below it Purbright noticed the incongruous presence of playroom relics – a bagatelle board, a tied bundle of toy rails, a battered magic lantern.

He looked up from these to see Warlock stooped in one of his now familiar sinuous postures and to hear: 'This household certainly seems well stocked with hammers. One for each job.'

Purbright peered over Warlock's shoulder. Lying in shadow along a wall beam about a foot from the floor was a hammer almost identical with the one found in the bathroom. Warlock pointed to faintly glistening fragments on its head. 'This is what must have been used to bust up the carboy, squire.' He turned upon the inspector a look compounded of satisfaction and expectancy; Purbright, surfeited with clues for one day, had the odd fancy that if he grasped and threw the hammer Warlock would leap, snap unerringly upon it in mid air, and with canine idiocy lay it again before him.

'Looks like it,' Purbright said, flatly.

Warlock whipped out a very clean handkerchief and picked up the hammer by the end of its haft. Holding it suspended before him, he slowly stood up and regarded it, frowning.

'I wonder why he didn't bring the other one down and use that. I'd have thought it was a pretty natural thing to do.'

'Squeamishness?' suggested Purbright.

'On his showing up to now you could hardly put him down as a sensitive type. Another thing – why should he have left these things about, anyway? He went to the trouble of smashing the carboy and burying it. Me, I'd have chucked the hammer in as well. Every time.'

Purbright smiled, a little wearily. 'Murdering people, Mr Warlock, must be a somewhat distracting business. Even the most conscientious practitioner probably tends to overlook things.'

As they re-entered the kitchen, there came from somewhere outside the house a short cooing call, soon afterwards repeated. The inspector went to the window and looked out.

Boggan, one foot on his spade, was turned towards the right-hand fence. A woman, apparently standing on something on her side of it, beckoned him eagerly. Boggan strolled across the lawn and listened to what she had to say. She was, Purbright noticed, an elderly woman, but rosy-faced and alert. For as long as she was talking she tilted back her head and kept her eyes tight shut, while her hand occasionally sought to discipline a stray wisp of her almost white hair.

Boggan sought the inspector.

'It's Mrs Sayers next door, sir. She'd like a word with you. She says she can tell you about Mr Periam.'

Chapter Three

MRS ALICE SAYERS celebrated the installation of a police inspector in her drawing-room by serving a jug of hot milk and water mixture delicately tinctured with coffee essence, switching on an electric fire that produced a cinematic representation of flames and a terrible smell of singeing fluff, and unshrouding the cage of a budgerigar called Trevor.

Also offered was a plate of slightly soft wheatmeal biscuits.

Purbright sat in a massive but unyielding armchair and watched Mrs Sayers administer fragments of biscuit to Trevor. This she did with a pout and a curious chuffling, sucking noise that was apparently intended to whet the bird's appetite.

At intervals she turned her head and with closed eyes addressed herself to the second most important creature in the room.

'I do hope you'll not think I'm just being terribly inquisitive, inspector, but I'm really very fond of Gordon and of course I didn't know what to think when I saw policemen all over the place. Well, people do fear the worst when it comes to *digging*, don't they?'

Her eyes opened and stayed watchful while she smiled, waiting to see how much she would be told.

'There's no need to let that alarm you, Mrs Sayers. All we know at the moment is that the two gentlemen next door appear to be … unaccounted for. There may be a perfectly simple explanation, but so long as there's the possibility of something being wrong we shall have to cast around a bit.'

Trevor, neglected, emitted a stream of staccato squawking that sounded like enamel being chiselled off a saucepan bottom. Purbright shivered. Mrs Sayers lovingly tapped the bars of the cage with her fingernail and reached for another biscuit.

'What you mean, I suppose, is that Gordon's missing? But how extraordinary. Couldn't he be on holiday, or something?'

'That is what we should very much like to know. When I received your message, I was hopeful that you might be able to tell us something definite.'

'Oh, naturally I shall do all I can to help, inspector. Mrs Periam was a very dear friend of mine. And Gordon was a crutch to her; I can't think of any other word. I wonder …' She paused. 'Have you by any chance had a word with Mrs Wilson? She's next to the Periams on the other side.'

'We did make some inquiries there. She wasn't able to tell us much.'

Mrs Sayers gave a quick satisfied nod. 'No, Mrs Wilson keeps pretty well to herself.' She thought again. 'Then there's Mrs Cork and her Miriam. They overlook at the back, you know. Have you tried them?'

'We shall bear them in mind,' Purbright said, patiently. Trevor hooted and began to peck at his perch in a sudden transport of paranoia. 'Choodle scrmsh,' murmured Mrs Sayers.

'Mr Periam has lived in the house next door all his life, I take it.'

'Oh, yes; he was born there. I remember how relieved we all were. She'd had a terrible time with him. Dr Peters wouldn't let her stir for the last four months. She lived on arrowroot and tonic wine and a woman called Dursnip or something like that used to call every Tuesday and Friday to massage the water up out of her legs. Of course, having babies nowadays is a dreadfully off-hand business, isn't it?'

'Relatively so,' confirmed Purbright.

'And yet she used to say to me that Gordon had made up for all she'd gone through and more besides. Every time he did some little thing for her she'd say that was another jewel God would put in his crown. She was a bit religious, you know. Well, I think it helped her when she lost her husband. Mastoid. Gordon wore a scarf every time he went out, winter and summer, right up to being nineteen or twenty. She was afraid it might have been passed on, but I think you can make too much of these things don't you?'

'Mr Periam wa ... isn't married?'

Mrs Sayers pouted and drew in a quick breath of denial.

'Girl friends?'

Mrs Sayers considered. 'There is a young lady who calls sometimes. I'd always supposed she belonged to the other one – Mr Hopjoy, you know; I think he's more that sort. But I wouldn't swear to it. Gordon's losing his mother might have made a difference.'

'Was Mr Periam on good terms with Mr Hopjoy? You've never heard them fall out with each other?'

'No, I haven't. Gordon has a sunny nature, though; I'm sure he'd get on with anyone. I'd call him staunch, too. Mind, between ourselves, the lodger's a bit of a fly-by-night. It says a lot for Gordon that he's let him stay on. I think it's because he feels his mother would have expected him to.'

'Mrs Periam thought well of Mr Hopjoy, then?'

Mrs Sayers gave the sort of smile with which one forgives the follies of the dead. 'She saw only the good in everyone.'

Trevor, now tramping rhythmically on his perch, cackled derisively. Mrs Sayers held up a finger, inviting Purbright's attention to the oracle. 'Get me serviette, mother; get me serviette, mother,' she translated. 'Well, I never,' said the inspector.

After an interval he deemed long enough to signify admiration, Purbright resumed his questioning.

'Do you happen to know who owns the car that's garaged next door?'

'Oh, yes, that's Mr Hopjoy's. Is it there now?'

'Not at the moment. When did you last see it, Mrs Sayers?'

'About a week ago, I should think. I can't say just …' She frowned. 'It's a biggish car. Beige. And ever so quiet.' She opened her eyes to see if the inspector would accept this information as a substitute for what he had wanted to know.

'But you can't remember – to a day or so, even – when you saw it last. And who was driving it.'

She shook her head. 'I'm not awfully observant of cars. And of course they both drive it a good deal; I suppose Mr Hopjoy lends it when he doesn't want it for his work.'

'I see. Now, Mrs Sayers, I'm going to ask you to think back very carefully to last Thursday just one week ago today. Does anything happen on Thursdays that might fix one in your mind?'

'Well, there's the laundry ... and the Brains Trust on television ...' She paused, seemingly unable to peer past so notable a peak, then suddenly patted her knee. 'Thursday – yes, I remember last Thursday; of course I do. It was Thursday that Arnold arrived. My second brother. He called on his way down from Hull.'

'Fine. Now try going over in your mind what happened that day – from one thing to the next, you know – and see if anything links up with next door. Never mind whether it seems important or not. Start right from getting up in the morning.'

Mrs Sayers, benignly co-operative, folded her hands and launched into a meticulous description of a day in the life of a Flaxborough widow. She spoke for nearly twenty minutes. Purbright learned, among many, many other things, three facts of possible relevance to his inquiry. On opening the door to take in the milk, Mrs Sayers had noticed Gordon Periam bolting back his gates. Some sixteen hours later, just before making up her brother's bed, she had looked down from the spare bedroom window to see Mr Hopjoy's car draw up. Gordon Periam – she was almost sure it was Gordon – got out and began unlocking the garage door. Finally, Mrs Sayers recalled a little vaguely having been awakened by the shutting of a door – that of the garage, she thought – and hearing a car with a quiet engine drive away. She did not know at what time this happened, but she had the impression that it was two or three o'clock on the Friday morning.

Purbright felt that Mrs Sayers's mind, such as it was, had been thoroughly worked out. But he made a last few random borings.

'Have you at any time recently, seen a big heavy package being carried into Mr Periam's?'

She had not.

'Since last Thursday, do you happen to have heard a noise like glass breaking? Next door, I mean.'

'There hasn't been a sound from there all this past week, inspector. Not a sound.' She stared at him, for the first time looking afraid. 'Well, they've been away, haven't they?'

'It seems they have, yes.' Purbright regarded absently a complicated bronze affair on the mantelpiece. It depicted an anxious nude heaving at the reins of a horse that had been maddened apparently by the grafting of a gilt clock to its belly. 'That's nearly ten minutes fast,' explained Mrs Sayers. Purbright, fearful of inviting a history of the bronze, looked quickly away.

He said: 'The bathroom next door … it's on the farther side of the house, I notice. Would any of the neighbours have a view of its window?'

'Well, only from the back, I should say. The houses in Pawson's Lane; that's where the ladies I told you about live. Mrs Cork and her daughter.'

'Would you say that they are inclined to be …' he paused, glancing at his palm … 'interested in people around here?'

'Miriam's drattedly nosey, if that's what you mean.'

'To the extent of writing anonymous letters?' Purbright saw a grin of gratification pouch Mrs Sayers's pink face. 'Ah,' she said, 'you've had one of those, have you?' She puffed out her lips and accompanied her speech with a slight shaking of her head: 'Yes, oh well, I knew ages ago that she'd got to the scribbling stage.' She lowered her voice and added mysteriously: 'The Change, you know.'

'She isn't a bit off the beam, is she?'

'Goodness me, no! Perfectly level-headed. And no harm in her, really. I think she just hasn't enough to do. She never had.' Again the voice plunged confidentially. 'Properly speaking and if all were told, inspector, the mother is *Miss* Cork. Miriam's illegit.'

Mrs Sayers, satisfied as a blood donor, leaned slowly back in her chair. 'I'm dying to know what Miriam wrote to you about. Do tell me.'

The inspector smiled apologetically. 'We did receive a letter, Mrs Sayers. I think there's no harm in your knowing that. It alleged some sort of a disturbance at number fourteen. The bathroom was mentioned. But I don't know that we can assume who wrote it.'

'We can put two and two together, though, can't we?'

'Ah, Mrs Sayers, if all the twos put together in this town had proved fertile we should be overrun with fours. I'm afraid I have been keeping you from your lunch.' He moved the ashtray with which Mrs Sayers had supplied him, a china representation of a Dutch clog, from his chair arm to the coffee table, and stood up. 'There's just one thing ...'

Mrs Sayers looked round for Trevor's cage cover. 'Yes?'

'I was wondering if you happened to know where we might pick up a photograph of Mr Periam. There are one or two portraits next door, but I don't suppose he's a choir-boy any longer.'

Mrs Sayers held up a promissory finger, pondered a moment, and trotted out of the room.

Trevor, still untented, immediately became hysterical. He nodded violently, issuing a series of high-frequency squawks that produced in Purbright the sensation of piano wires being jerkily reeled in through his ears. He tried to imitate Mrs Sayers's method of soothing communion but this merely agitated the bird more. He made faces at it, growled, miaowed, muttered words of the kind that are passed to magistrates on slips of paper. Trevor's slate-pencil monody persisted. In a final attempt, Purbright drew desperately on his cigarette and filled the cage with smoke. He was rewarded immediately. The bird swayed a little, raised one claw, then hunched into immobility and utter silence.

Purbright was standing by the window with his back to the fumigated budgerigar when Mrs Sayers bustled in with a photograph.

'Here we are: this was taken at last year's Operatic. *The Student Prince*. That's Gordon – the one holding up the beer mug thing in the second row.'

Purbright examined the picture. It showed upwards of thirty members of the Flaxborough Amateur Operatic Society transfixed in self-conscious attitudes of Ruritanian abandon. There was a wealth of false mustachios, arms akimbo, flourished steins, peasant blouses ('I helped with the costumes,' proclaimed Mrs Sayers) and feet on chairs. A drinking song was clearly in progress. In the foreground was a pair whom Purbright assumed to be the principals of the show. Disguised as a prince disguised as a student, forty-eight-year-old Jack Bottomley, bachelor proprietor of the Freemasons' Arms, accompanied his singing with a stiff, resolute gesture; he looked like a learner driver about to turn left. His other hand grasped the waist of the Society's perennial soprano lead, Miss Hilda Cannon, a stick-like female whose desperate grin of simulated coquetry was belied by the angle at which she leaned away from the draught of Mr Bottomley's romantic protestations ...

'No, no; *that* one's Gordon.' Mrs Sayers's plump little finger redirected Purbright's attention to the face in the second row.

It was an unexceptional face that he could not recall having seen before, although, as Periam was a shop-keeper in a fairly busy part of the town, it was more than likely that he had done so. The features were very smooth, like those of an elderly baby, and their sulky solemnity was emphasized by a big, round, fleshy chin. The posture of gaiety prescribed for the occasion had been adopted by Mr Periam with all the insouciance of a man with suspected rib fractures submitting to X-ray examination.

'He doesn't look very happy,' Purbright ventured.

'A terribly conscientious boy,' Mrs Sayers explained. 'Actually he has a lovely sense of fun, but in a quiet way. He's not one for roystering about. I think it's only loyalty, really, that's kept him in things like this. He's still a regular Gang Show man too, you know.'

'Does Mr Hopjoy go in for theatricals?'

Mrs Sayers puffed contemptuously. 'Not on the stage, he doesn't. But he's an actor, all right, take it from me.'

'I'd rather like his picture as well.'

'I don't know where you'll get one. By all accounts he flits around too much to be photographed. Of course, some woman might help you there. Or even,' she added darkly, 'the police.'

Purbright, pocketing the photograph of the Operatic Society, searched her face for evidence either of amnesia or an unexpected sense of humour.

'No, honestly,' Mrs Sayers soberly persisted, 'it wouldn't surprise me one little bit.'

Chapter Four

Towards conference with the Chief Constable of Flaxborough and one selected senior officer of his force smoothly sped the man known as Ross.

He gazed with languid appreciation through the windscreen of the Bentley – an ordinary Bentley save that its radiator cowl was of gunmetal and of slightly more assertive radius than a standard model's – at the June countryside. He already had booked rooms for his companion and himself at the Royal Oak, Flaxborough, from a public call box on the road from London, using the names Smith – his own favourite among disarmingly improbable hotel aliases – and Pargetter.

Pargetter-to-be did not seem to be enjoying the drive as much as Ross. As the long car swung up from the last declivity in the wooded, river-watered lowlands below Flaxborough Ridge and gained the straight highway leading to the town, he shifted irritably in his seat and swivelled his head in an effort to read grass-collared milestones.

Ross did not care for the back view of his companion's head; the gleam of baldness bobbed distractingly in the left corner of his vision and he had begun to receive the curious impression that it emanated from a beard-ringed featureless face.

'Harry,' he said sharply, 'what on earth are you looking for?'

The white patch disappeared and a sallow oval one took its place. 'I've been trying to see how much farther we have to go. I think there was a three on that last milestone.'

Henry Pumphrey spoke rapidly but with a careful emphasis that involved his facial muscles in a good deal of exercise. At the end of each sentence he lightly flicked his tongue across his upper lip. He had a residual North Country accent.

'Three miles will be about it,' Ross agreed. He had glanced at the dashboard and received from it, apparently, information no less precise than Pumphrey's. Now, his hands laid delicately upon the wheel as upon an open missal, he watched the gradual recession of trees and hedges from the road ahead and their replacement by houses, a filling station, some shops. Cyclists – Flaxborough cyclists who seem grafted to their machines to form unities as formidable and unpredictable as centaurs – swooped out of side roads. Green double-decked buses which had been ticking over in ambush loomed suddenly at intersections. With the serenity of extreme old age, three inmates of an almshouse crossed and re-crossed the carriageway, gently smiled resignation to survival for another twenty-four hours, and filed back into their refuge. A pair of dogs, panting and oblivious, coupled on the road's crown and performed a six-legged waltz around a keep-left bollard. Children darted between cars and laid down objects which they then watched excitedly from the pavement.

All these hazards were negotiated with smooth synchronisation by the Bentley, presided over by Ross. He remained calm, indulgent, interested.

Just short of a large, pale blue sign mounted on posts, Ross drew the car to a halt. At his request Pumphrey wound down the window on his side and Ross leaned across him, calling to the squat, sceptical looking man who lounged against one of the sign's supports.

'I say, I wonder if you could tell me in which part of the town I can find the police headquarters.'

The man silently regarded the casual balance of the traveller's forward-thrust shoulder, its suiting of hand-blended Newbiggin wool and linen dyed to the colour of Chartres Cathedral, the musicianly hands that sprang so surprisingly from wrists as powerful as a road driller's. He shifted his glance to Ross's face; a patient face, not very handsome, the face of a questioner and connoisseur, a trader – in the last resort – of pain.

When the man's slow scrutiny reached Ross's eyes he saw they were lifted to absorb the message of the tall, clean lettering above them. FLAXBOROUGH WELCOMES CAREFUL DRIVERS.

The man politely awaited the descent of Ross's gaze before he carefully cleared his throat and spoke.

'Piss off,' he said.

*

The Chief Constable of Flaxborough, Mr Harcourt Chubb, received his London visitors with a degree of affability that he calculated would fall just short of making them feel entitled to put him to any trouble. He introduced

Purbright, who found Ross's handshake a shade prolonged and somewhat exploratory, and Pumphrey's over-firm, like that of a man for ever determined to make his first friend.

All but Mr Chubb sat down. He stepped back and relaxed his tall, lean body against the mantelpiece, with one arm extended along it.

Ross glanced at him, then at Purbright.

'I assume, inspector, that Mr Chubb has explained the nature of our interest in this little affair of yours at ... Flaxborough.' The small hesitation was eloquent of the orientation difficulties of the much travelled. Perhaps the day before it had been Istanbul or Adelaide that needed to be slotted into some similar interview.

Purbright inclined his head. 'I do understand that one of these missing people, a man called Hopjoy, happens to be ...'

'... One of our fellows, yes.' Ross completed the identification with brisk despatch, then looked intently at Purbright. 'Of course, you see how we might be placed?'

'Not precisely, sir.'

Pumphrey's cheek twitched with disapproval of the provincial policeman's obtuseness. 'It simply means that, security-wise ...' He stopped and turned his eyes, like those of an El Greco Christ, upon Ross.

Ross smiled patiently. 'Thimble Bay. Let's start from there, shall we? I don't have to tell you about the Thimble Bay Establishment. Couldn't, anyway – not above Sensitivity Three, and you wouldn't be much wiser if I did. But you'll understand the place is very much our pigeon. Hence Hopjoy. Among others, naturally.'

'That much I had gathered,' Purbright said. 'Of course, Thimble Bay is not usually considered to be in this locality, sir.'

'Really?' Ross sounded surprised. He glanced across at the Chief Constable, as a misled traveller might appeal direct to the king of the country whose inhabitants have proved wayward. 'How far, Mr Chubb, would you say Thimble Bay is from here?'

The Chief Constable deficiently waved one of his fine flexible, hands. 'I really can't tell you. Mr Purbright will know.'

'Twenty-seven miles, sir.'

A little puff of disparagement issued from Pumphrey's black, up-tilted nostrils. 'Well, that may seem a long way to you, inspector, but, good heavens, globe-wise ...'

'My colleague,' Ross broke in, 'doesn't mean to sound like an astronomer. We do appreciate that you have quite enough on your plate without worrying about what goes on a couple of counties away. It's just that we have to take rather long views in our job.' He gave a sudden placatory grin and drew a cigarette case from an inner pocket. 'Tell me, do you find time to play cricket, inspector?'

'No, sir,' replied Purbright, no less pleasantly.

For a fraction of a second the pressure of Ross's thumb on a catch of the cigarette case was arrested. Then he completed the movement and offered a cigarette first to Mr Chubb, who pursed bis lips in refusal, and then to Purbright. Pumphrey seemed not to qualify.

'The reason I ask,' Ross went on, is this. Picture Thimble Bay as the wicket. Security is simply a matter of placing fielders. You know, slips, cover-point, silly mid-off, square check ...'

'I don't play lacrosse either, sir,' murmured Purbright.

'Square check,' repeated Ross. 'Wrong game. Yes, you're perfectly right. Full marks.' He leaned back in his chair, crossing his legs. 'But you've caught on, haven't you, to what I mean about fielding. Hopjoy – we'll call him that – was our Flaxborough longstop, so to speak.'

Purbright digested the metaphor, with which Ross was looking very satisfied. 'His job, then, was to intercept such information as happened to leak in this direction.' He turned to the Chief Constable. 'I had no idea we were on a spying route; had you, sir?'

'Certainly not,' said Mr Chubb. 'This isn't ...' – he sought a sufficiently preposterous location – 'Algiers or ... or Dublin.'

Ross carefully tapped the ash from his cigarette. 'You know Dublin, Mr Chubb?' he inquired of the ashtray.

'I can't say that I do. Why?'

'The name seemed to occur to you.'

'Oh, that. Well. Roger Casement and everything ... association of ideas, I suppose.' To his bewilderment Mr Chubb found himself thinking defensively. He closed his mouth firmly and glanced up at the office clock.

Pumphrey seemed about to slip in a supplementary question but Ross, suddenly benign, reached over and took from his lap the briefcase he had been nursing. 'This,' he explained to Purbright, 'is pretty sensitive stuff. You'll appreciate that I can't let you right into the picture, but these reports from Hopjoy do suggest that he might have been on to something.'

He took from his pocket a number of coins and selected what appeared to be an ordinary florin. 'Special knurling,' he observed, indicating the coin's rim. Then he slipped it into a slot in the otherwise featureless lock of the case and turned it carefully. Purbright guessed that the fine-toothed rim was engaging a tiny gear within the lock. After a second or two there was a click and the flap of the case hung open.

Ross drew out a slim sheaf of papers and began glancing through them without disturbing their order. Purbright caught sight of a couple of maps and a number of smaller sheets that appeared to be accounts. The rest of the papers bore closely-spaced typing, neatly indented and with underlined sub-headings. 'Most meticulous chap,' Ross murmured.

The Chief Constable shifted his position slightly and rubbed his chin with two fingers. 'We realize,' he said, 'that Mr Hopjoy was engaged on somewhat delicate work involving matters that do not concern us as ordinary policemen. What does concern us, though, is the probability of a crime having been committed. Let me be quite frank, gentlemen: to what extent are we going to be able to collaborate in sorting this business out?'

Ross looked a little surprised. 'Fully I trust, Mr Chubb. That is why Mr Pumphrey and I are here – to be kept informed with the least inconvenience to you.'

It was Chubb's turn to raise his brows. 'I had hoped for something rather more reciprocal, Mr Ross.' He looked meaningfully at the Hopjoy file. 'If it turns out that your man was done away with, the answer might very well lie there.'

'That's true.' There was a note of doubt in Ross's voice. 'The trouble is that this stuff hasn't been processed thoroughly yet. Our people gave it a preliminary feed through R Section but the report wasn't terribly suggestive. All Hopjoy's leads are green. Linkage negative. Well …' He shrugged and gave Pumphrey a glance that invited confirmation of their difficulties. Pumphrey responded with a judicial nod.

The inspector, who had been listening with polite attention, asked: 'What are green leads, Mr Ross?'

'And negative linkages?' threw in Chubb, without sounding in the least curious.

Ross beamed. The sudden smile invested his large, rather lumpishly cast face with a charm that was the greater for being unexpected, like greenery on a pit heap. 'I'm sorry about the technicalities,' he said. 'A green lead is what you might call a new suspect, someone with no history of unreliability.'

'Very tricky,' observed Pumphrey, joining the tips of his long hair-backed fingers.

'And by linkage negative,' Ross went on, 'we mean that the person in question can't be shown to have contact with any other bad security risks. Of course, it's only a matter of time before we put that right: no one can keep to himself indefinitely. There's the chance meeting in a pub, membership of the same library, connections dating back to schooldays ... oh, lord, we can trace them, don't you worry.'

Ross pressed out the stub of his cigarette, on which he had drawn scarcely at all since lighting it, and took from his pocket a long, slim pipe with a squat, highly-polished bowl. This he filled carefully, holding it close against his stomach, from a pouch of Andalusian doeskin (which honey curing makes the softest hide in the world). Between studied applications of the match flame, he tamped down the pure Latakia with a small metal ram. Seeing Purbright's interest, Ross waited until the tobacco glowed securely then tossed the object across to him.

Purbright rolled the still hot cylinder around his cupped palm. It was a little under an inch long and consisted of half a dozen tiny discs or washers clamped together by a central screw. Half the discs were copper and the remainder of some white metal. The two kinds were set alternately.

'A momento of the Lubianka,' Ross said. He stared straight ahead over the pipe bowl and rhythmically released portentous pops of smoke from the corner of his mouth. Then he stretched to reclaim the cylinder from Purbright.

'When this,' he said, 'is slipped into a hole drilled in one of a man's vertebrae, a galvanic reaction is set up between the dissimilar metals. By the time the wound heals, a constant electric current is being fed into his spinal cord. The secret police call the spasms of his death agony the Gold and Silver Waltz.'

The strained silence that ensued was broken by the Chief Constable, who inquired if Mr Ross was prepared to do any interviewing in Flaxborough in pursuit of whatever line of investigation seemed suggested in the reports of the missing agent.

Ross squeezed a noise of assent past his pipe stem then removed and examined it. 'I was going to ask you,' he said, 'just how amenable to questioning I might expect to find the people around here.'

'What is their co-operation-potential?' Pumphrey translated.

'A very decent lot, by and large,' replied Mr Chubb, 'if you know how to handle them.'

'Oh, well, that's all right, then.' Ross decided against citing the unencouraging example of the man he had asked the way to the police station. 'For a start, perhaps you'd better tell us how you see this business, Purbright. Any ideas?'

The inspector, answering without haste, gazed directly but mildly at Ross's face. This now wore an expression of eager courtesy – that look which is only a polite version of imperiousness.

'Beyond the not particularly intelligent deduction that someone was murdered in that house and his body disposed of,' Purbright began, 'I can't pretend to having much to offer. Not even the fact of murder can be confirmed until the laboratory reports come through although, as I say, I haven't much doubt of it. Then the question of identity will have to be settled. We are in no position at the moment to say who killed whom. Naturally, we assume the choice lies between the owner of the house, Periam, and your man Hopjoy. You, sir, might have reasons of your own for supposing Hopjoy to be the more likely candidate ...'

'Not necessarily,' Ross broke in. 'Our chaps are fairly adept at looking after themselves, you know. We give them credit for that.'

'You mean you would not be surprised to find that it was Periam who was killed?'

'In my job, Purbright, we soon lose all capacity for being surprised.'

'But if Hopjoy was responsible ...'

'Then he must have had some very compelling reason.' Ross removed his pipe and squinted along its stem. 'Mind you, I think that possibility is unlikely. I'm not aware that Hopjoy had any general authorisation to take executive decisions. On the other hand, I shouldn't necessarily have been informed if he had.'

'Well, that's helpful, I must say,' said the Chief Constable. 'Don't any of you chaps know what you're up to?' Flushing slightly, he straightened and stood clear of the mantelpiece. 'Four years ago I received a confidential request to give this fellow Hopjoy co-operation if he asked for it and not to bother him if he didn't. Fair enough. As it happens, he never came to us for anything. But there were one or two occasions when we were able to smooth things out for him in little ways behind the scenes. There was no fuss, no gossip, nothing.' Chubb spread his hands and nodded. 'All right, we were just doing our duty. But now' – he jabbed a finger in Ross's direction – 'it looks as if something has happened that can't be glossed over. Something absolutely intolerable. And you must realise, Mr Ross, that I have no intention of allowing my officers to temper their efforts to solve this crime with consideration for what you may regard as higher policy.'

Purbright, who had been examining his finger-ends while marvelling at the length and vehemence of Chubb's speech, looked up blandly at Ross. It was Pumphrey, though, who spoke first.

'It seems to me, Mr Chubb, that you don't quite understand that this business involves security.' The final word leaped from the rest of the tightly controlled sentence like a whippet trying to break its leash.

Ross, still amiable and matter-of-fact, gave a quick, chairman-like glance round the others, reserving for the Chief Constable a smile that promised concession. 'No,' he said, 'that's not altogether fair. Mr Chubb appreciates that this affair has certain delicate features, but a crime's a crime and he's perfectly right to view this one from the standpoint of the very good policeman we all know him to be. Of course the investigation must proceed in the way he thinks best. Major Pumphrey and I ask only that we be allowed to assist with what specialized knowledge we have.'

Like a peal proclaiming a peace treaty, the ringing of the telephone on Chubb's desk provided a distraction from uncharitable thoughts. At a nod from the Chief Constable, Purbright took the call.

When he replaced the receiver he thrust a hand beneath his jacket, scratched himself gently, and announced: 'The car's been traced, anyway. At the moment it's parked in the Neptune yard at Brockleston. It might be as well if I nipped over there now, don't you think, sir?'

Chapter Five

THE THIRTY-MILE DRIVE to Brockleston brought Purbright into the town's main street at exactly five o'clock, when it looked like a row of aquarium tanks.

Staring out at him from behind the windows of the twenty-three cafés and snack bars were the perplexed, hostile eyes of holiday-makers awaiting the fish and chips, pies and chips, ham and chips, egg and chips, sausage and chips – in fact, every permutation of succulence except chips and chips – that were being borne to their plastic-topped tables by girls with corded necks and dress seams strained to the limit as they ferried their great trays.

Brockleston was a day trippers' resort. Its resident population, no greater than that of a village, occupied a string of timber bungalows on the lee side of the dunes or lived in the flats above the few shops not associated with the chips industry. There were no boarding houses, for the ephemeral pleasures of the place did not justify a protracted visit. The dunes, while adequate for desultory, gritty fornication, served no other purpose than mercifully to screen a muddy beach from which jutted derelict anti-tank blocks. The sea at most times was an afternoon's march away.

Yet it was the sea, distinctly visible as a glinting streak of silver beyond the steamy, creek-veined plain, and therefore an object of pilgrimage, that accounted for all the coming and going along the Flaxborough road, the seasonal cramming of the twenty-three cafés and two small pubs, and the enforced but bitterly begrudged construction by the rural council of a public convenience whose necessarily ample proportions had earned it the local epithet of the Taj Mahal.

The Neptune Hotel represented a totally different tradition.

It had been erected only five years previously by a Flaxborough jobbing builder whose coincidental relationship with the chairman of the housing committee had put him in the way of contracts for five estates of bay-windowed rabbit hutches and made the chairman the brother-in-law of a millionaire. The Neptune was now as valuable a property as any three hotels in Flaxborough put together.

There may have been something a little Victorian about the Flaxbrovians' propensity to translate a novelty into a fashion and a fashion into a steady habit, but the creator of the Neptune saw no point in derogating any trend from which he might capitalise. He knew his fellow citizens, Victorian or no, and was concerned, as he put it, only with what they would 'go for'.

'You know, Lizz,' he had said to his housekeeper one night, 'they're a rum lot of buggers in Flax. They like to get the hell out of the place to enjoy themselves, but all the same old faces have to be there at the other end when they arrive. Even when they just want to tread each other's missuses once in a while, damn me if they find any fun in it unless they can say how d'ye do to the women's husbands on the stairs. They pretend not to be sociable, but that's just a pose, you know, Lizz. What I reckon they want is a place right off the track where they can be sociable in private. Here, gal, pass us that map a minute ... it's on the table there, just by your pillow ...'

Thus had the Neptune been conceived.

Its progenitor had not attempted the actual construction himself but had entrusted it to a competent builder whose tenders for the Council estates he had always managed to underquote and on whom, therefore, he felt constrained to bestow a measure of compensatory patronage.

The hotel was an imposing building, four storeys high and with a glass tower at one corner. In this tower sat a huge robot fashioned in neon tubing, a mechanical celebrant that raised at regular intervals a glowing tankard and pledged good cheer to the surrounding acres of empty sea and marsh. The only people who considered it merely vulgar were those who wouldn't have spent much in the hotel anyway and therefore didn't matter; the rest, eagerly seeking from their Brockleston-bound cars a first glimpse of the roysterer in the sky, thought it a marvel of cleverness that reflected great credit on one and all, including, naturally, themselves.

At the hour when Purbright drove into the great concrete forecourt of the Neptune (his earlier reference to it as a 'yard' had been in deference to the Chief Constable's known contempt for the modern conceits of the licensing trade) the entowered automaton was not working. He was able to appreciate, however, the other, only slightly less impressive features of the building: the dawn-pink façade pointed with black asterisks, the candy-striped sun awnings, the sculpted representation of nude nymphs playing leapfrog before the main entrance itself – a shallow but wide portico framing two immense concave plates of heavy glass, counter-sprung to yield to the touch of the most diffident venturer into high life.

Purbright parked the rather shabby police car beside half a dozen much grander vehicles already standing in the forecourt. One of them, he noticed, bore the number plate which had been identified by a Brockleston constable – presumably the florid-faced youngster in uniform whom Purbright spotted in an attitude of assumed and unconvincing nonchalance against the far wall of the court.

Gently elbowing open one of the glass plates, Purbright crossed a quarter-acre of bottle-green carpet to the reception counter. Beyond and seemingly below this formidable rampart sat a girl whose shoulders moved with the rhythm of knitting. At the inspector's approach, she raised a small, melancholy, and mistrustful face.

'Yes?' She glanced back at her needles.

'I should like a word with the manager, if he's available.'

'Mr Barraclough?' The girl seemed not to deem Purbright worth a second look.

'Yes, if that's his name.'

'I'll see if he's in.' She knitted on to the end of the row, thrust the wool into some recess below the counter, and rose. Purbright was a little startled by the revelation of silk-encased thighs. The girl's costume, evidently intended to transform her into a stimulating replica of an American night club attendant, proved in fact a bizarre detraction from whatever charm she might have had. As she walked indolently to a door at the end of the counter her flesh wobbled within the incongrous tights with as much sexual provocation as a blancmange on a waiter's trolley.

Purbright turned and gazed gloomily round the big empty reception hall, shadowlessly aglow with the light from orange opalescent panels in the ceiling. There were three tall doors, black and thinly striped with gold and pierced with clear glass portholes, set in each of the side walls; they led, he supposed, to bars and lounges. The hall funnelled gently at its opposite end to a broad staircase. The apparent absence of a lift puzzled Purbright at first. Then a plunging purr of deceleration drew his eye to what he had taken to be a round supporting pillar in the very centre of the hall. It split and opened like the rind of some Arabian Nights fruit and disgorged a tubby man with a professional smile and rather a lot of cuff. As he walked briskly towards Purbright he gave the curious impression of paddling himself along on his elbows. He stopped just short of a collision. 'Sar!'

Purbright raised his eyebrows and glanced from the man to the stalagmite lift shaft. 'The genie of the lamp?'

The man's smile remained tightly screwed on, but the rest of his facial furniture shifted slightly; he obviously did not care for levity. 'Or Mr Barraclough, rather,' Purbright corrected himself.

The manager nodded and rested one hand on the counter, behind which the leggy receptionist had silently reappeared.

Purbright handed him a card. 'I should like,' he said, 'to verify the presence in your hotel of a gentleman who may be able to help me with a few inquiries.'

'One of the staff?'

'I think it more likely that he is among your guests, sir.'

The manager's momentary expression of anxiety faded. At that time of year customers were much more readily expendable than employees. He turned to the girl. 'The register, please, Dorabel.'

'There is one minor complication,' said Purbright. 'I do not precisely know the man's name' – Barraclough shrugged and seemed about to countermand his request for the register – 'but never mind, I can give you the choice of two.'

The manager's suspicion deepened that this tall, smart-aleck policeman was making faintly menacing jokes as a prelude to extorting an offer of free drink. He ran through quickly in his mind those most recent instances of malfeasance at the Neptune which might conceivably have come to the notice of authority.

'I hope,' he said, taking an opulently bound volume from the arms of Dorabel, 'that these inquiries of yours won't cause trouble of any kind. Mistakes aren't too easy to put right once they're made.' That part of his brain that had been sifting the possible reasons for the inspector's arrival struck suddenly upon a lantern lecture given the previous Wednesday night in one of the private lounges to a Flaxborough Chamber of Trade party. A slide discovered among the bottles the next morning and brought to him by a distressed chambermaid had suggested a somewhat liberal exposition of the lecture's theme, 'Commercial Deviations in the Near East.'

'Perhaps you'd better come along to my office,' said Barraclough. He picked up the register and led Purbright through one of the black doors, a short way along a corridor and into a relatively austere cubicle that contained a filing cabinet, an untidy, old-fashioned desk and a stack of cartons of cigarettes. He reached towards a bellpush. 'You'll have a little refreshment, inspector?'

'That's kind of you, sir, but I don't really feel in need of any at the moment.'

To Barraclough such apparently eccentric asceticism was confirmative of even more serious matters being afoot than he had been able so far to imagine. He meekly invited Purbright to a chair and opened the register. 'Those two names?' he prompted.

'One of them is Hopjoy.'

Barraclough looked up sharply. 'What's he been up to?'

'You know Mr Hopjoy, then?'

'He's spent quite a bit of … time here. On and off, you know.' The information was delivered cautiously.

'A good spender? Other than of time.'

'We've always valued his custom, certainly. In this business one has to be accommodating on the odd occasion, of course. Mr Hopjoy has excellent credentials. Naturally I cannot divulge them, but I dare say they'd surprise you.'

Purbright recognised the nervous loyalty of a creditor. 'Do you happen to know,' he asked, 'Mr Hopjoy's occupation?'

For a moment, the manager hesitated. Then discretion won. 'He's an agent for some big manufacturing firm. An excellent position, I understand.'

'Is he staying here now, sir?'

Barraclough did not refer to the register. 'Not at the moment, he isn't. We haven't seen him for a few days. I should explain that he is not in the way of being a regular resident. Just the odd night – when he happens to be covering this district, I suppose.'

'Mr Hopjoy's car is outside now.'

Barraclough looked only faintly surprised. 'Yes? Well, I'm not absolutely certain about this but I should say it's on loan to a friend of his. I believe they do share it to some extent.' He paused, then asked, almost hopefully, Purbright thought: 'It is the car that these inquiries of yours are about?'

The inspector shrugged. 'Not primarily; though cars do tend to figure in all sorts of investigations these days – they're becoming our second skins, aren't they? No, it's the driver I really want to see. I presume he's a Mr Periam.'

'Mr Periam is staying here.'

'Do you know for how long?'

'Another week, I believe.'

'I should appreciate a word with him, sir. Perhaps if you can give me the number of his room ...'

Frowning, Barraclough reached for the telephone on his desk. 'I'd really rather you ... Dorabel, has Mr Periam in number eleven gone out yet? All right, dear; hold the line a moment ...' He put his hand over the mouthpiece. 'He's in his room. You can see him in here if you like – that would be best, wouldn't it?' Hurriedly he spoke again into the phone. 'Ask Mr Periam if he'd be good enough to come down; when he does, show him into my office.'

Barraclough sat back in his chair and flicked at his sleeve. 'I'm sorry if I seem a bit formal over this, inspector, but I'm assuming your business is confidential and I shouldn't like one of my guests to be embarrassed. He might be, you know, if you barged straight up to his room. And then there's Mrs Periam to be considered, of course.'

Purbright stared at the plump, watchful little man, who now had given his smile a wistful cast to suit the part of tactful paternalism. '*Mrs* Periam?'

'Oh, yes; a rather dear little thing. I'm sure you wouldn't want to spoil her honeymoon.'

Chapter Six

IN THE PRIVACY of a bedroom in an hotel a great deal less considerately appointed than was the Neptune for honeymooning or, indeed, any other purpose, Ross and Pumphrey considered a course of inquiry that was to be separate and, for a while at least, divergent from Purbright's.

Upon the decrepit bamboo table that divided Ross, seated in the only chair, and Pumphrey, perched on the thinly blanketed concrete slab that served as a bed, lay the file on Hopjoy's operational reports.

Neither man had referred to the Chief Constable's claim to be made privy of these papers. The well-meaning but gauche presumption of officers in the civil police were too familiar to be resented or even discussed.

Ross did, however, touch conversationally upon the personalities of those whom the disconcerting interruption of Line F.7 had made their temporary and tenuous associates. Mr Chubb he pronounced 'an odd old bird: I kept expecting him to ring for a butler to show us out. The Purbright I'm a shade doubtful about. There's a streak of cleverness there that doesn't go with a provincial copper. I suppose he's been cleared?'

'There's no R-rating compiled, actually, but I can find no minus entry against him later than 1936, so it seems he'd be entitled to a ninety-four or ninety-five. That's pretty average for police above sergeant.'

'1936 ... Left Book Club, I suppose?'

Pumphrey shook his head. 'Flaxborough Grammar School Debating Society: he did some sort of a skit on Stanley Baldwin, apparently.'

Ross took his pipe from his pocket and leaned forward over the typescript before him. He read in silence for several minutes.

Pumphrey sat immobile. His breathing was regular but each exhalation seemed to encounter some slight adenoidal constriction. In the small, quiet room, the noise was obtrusive. He sounded like a man patiently trying to cool a very hot dinner.

Flicking over a page, Ross increased the pace of his reading. Soon he was glancing from paragraph to paragraph as if refreshing his memory of already digested passages. The last couple of pages he absorbed whole. He leaned back in the angular, threadbare chair and stared thoughtfully into his pipe bowl. When he spoke, it was without looking up.

Pumphrey gave a start. 'Sorry, I didn't ...' He perked forward his pallid, sharp face and half-opened his mouth as though it were a third ear.

'I said he's kept it all pretty carefully wrapped up.'

'Naturally.'

'Yes, but it doesn't help us a great deal at the moment. He's been eleven days out of contact now ...'

'Twelve,' Pumphrey corrected.

'All right, twelve. That makes a takeover automatic. But we can't put another fellow in without some clarification.

Considering F.7 ran up some of the fattest exes in the sector I think it might have been left a bit tidier.'

Pumphrey eased another inch or two of neck out of his collar and stroked his chin. 'You don't suppose there's a tactical explanation, I take it? You feel sure he's been operationally negatived?'

'Oh, they've got him, all right. Rough luck on the poor devil, but we're not here to organise a wake. As long as we do our job of joining up the cut ends as quickly as possible we can leave the bobbies to worry about what they think is the crime angle. Our people will see that nothing's let out.'

'Suppose there's an arrest, though. And a trial.'

'Oh, I hope they get the swine; I do, indeed. All I'm saying is that we aren't primarily concerned with that aspect. And, believe me, if anyone is convicted it will be as plain Henry Jones, burglar, sadist, deceived husband, spurned queer – anything that a supremely efficient organisation can pull out of its bag to hide the true identity and motive of one of its operators who was unlucky enough to be caught.'

Ross carefully pocketed the doeskin pouch from which he had been shredding Latakia (black, he thought, as the gullet of that Transylvanian girl, rigid and love-groaning as his mouth descended upon hers in the Bucharest pullman ...). He struck a match and allowed the last vestige of sulphur in its head to be expelled before holding the clear-burning pine a quarter of an inch above the pipe bowl. As he sucked, the high yellow flame curtsied and sent blue tongues stabbing down into the tight stack of tobacco. The dark laminated strands heaved, separated and became fiery filaments, then grey stamens of ash upon a glowing corolla. Finally they were crushed down beneath the curious bi-metallic tamping ram. A blue cloud streamed parallel to the long stem, was divided by the bowl, bright as a horse chestnut newly split from its husk, and joined again in lazy assault upon the unappreciative nostrils of Pumphrey, who coughed pointedly and swung his head aside.

Ross regarded the manoeuvre without sympathy. 'You're no sensualist, Harry,' he reproved, mentally picturing Transylvanian frustration in the face of Pumphrey's aridity.

'The police,' said Pumphrey, sticking to what he conceived to be the point, 'are bound to consider that Periam is deeply implicated.'

'Periam?'

'The man Hopjoy lodged with.'

Ross shrugged. 'That doesn't mean a thing. We can be sure that our friends arranged for someone to appear implicated. There's nothing here to suggest that Periam really had anything to do with it.' He waved towards the file.

'Oh, no; Hopjoy was confident enough in him. M cross-checked, of course. Right up to Blue One.'

Ross raised his brows. 'What on earth did they suppose he was, a first sec?'

'It was perfectly reasonable, security-wise ...' Pumphrey paused to brace himself against another smoke cloud ... 'to put maximum screen on anyone sharing a house with one of our own operators. Periam cleared remarkably high, as it turned out. Even his relationship record was negative up to second cousin radius. Associative adulteration, nil. After allowance for stability depreciation he rings up a ninety-nine point six.'

'My God! He must be the only one.'

Pumphrey gave a slight shake of his head. 'There are sixteen, actually. Occupation-wise, the breakdown is interesting. Five of them are tobacconists, like Periam. I think market gardeners come next. The rest are fairly mixed.'

'Any archbishops?'

Pumphrey considered, frowning. 'No,' he said at last. 'I rather think not.' He looked up. 'I can check if you like. It's hardly relevant, though, is it?'

'Hardly.' Ross stretched his big, action-loving body, savouring the innocent ecstasy of muscular power at full rack until the shabby hotel chair whimpered and there glittered from the gold links on his upthrust wrists the tiny diamonds prised in 1952 (so Ross could have told, had he wished) from the front teeth of the flamboyant inquisitor and tormentor Spuratkin.

Ross let fall his arms, slumped happily for half a minute, then sat up straight and alert. 'We'd better make a start. All we can do at this stage is to follow Hopjoy's lines more or less at random until we get some sort of a picture. I suggest you begin with a haircut, Harry.'

'George Tozer,' Pumphrey responded with unwonted pertness, 'thirty-two Spindle Lane. Correct?'

Ross grinned and rose. 'Absolutely correct, old son.' He felt touched, as he did whenever Pumphrey allowed pride in his gift of fact-retention to glimmer through an otherwise sombre personality, and did not grudge acknowledgement. Daringly he added: 'Just as well the name's not Todd, eh?'

Pumphrey looked blank. 'Todd?' He unfolded a street map of Flaxborough, found Spindle Lane, and committed to memory the names of the intermediate roads. 'Todd?' he repeated, looking up.

'Nothing,' said Ross. 'Just a joke. A barber joke.' There was something, he reflected, a little Teutonic about Pumphrey.

A solitary fly patrolled the latticed shaft of sunshine that slanted down upon the hair-sprinkled brown linoleum of Mr Tozer's saloon. Its intermittent hum emphasized that silence, all but absolute, which is peculiar to barbers' shops on custom-less afternoons in summer. The air in the small room, low-ceilinged and set three steps below street level, was warm and sleepy with the scent of bay rum. A fresh slip of toilet tissue curled preparatorily across the neck rest of the shaving chair was as motionless as a marble scroll. The scissors, razors, and hand clippers set in methodic array at the back of the big oval wash-basin seemed as unlikely to be put ever again to use as tools sanguinely sealed into a burial chamber in Luxor.

Even the proprietor appeared to have undergone a necropolitan translation. He was sprawled peacefully across three cane-bottomed chairs beneath a row of hat pegs in an alcove, his head cushioned on a pile of tattered magazines and his hands crossed upon the folds of his white coat.

Pumphrey, having peered down through the window upon Mr Tozer's tonsorial tomb, was a little surprised to find the door unlocked. But at the instant of his entrance, which set jangling a little bell above the door, Mr Tozer rose stiffly and all of a piece, like a sleep walker, and advanced upon him holding out invitingly what a more fanciful caller might have taken to be a shroud.

The barber side-stepped to allow Pumphrey to subside into the chair, whipped the sheet round his neck and stood for a moment melancholically surveying the irregular vestiges of scrub upon the celery-white scalp.

'Haircut, sir?' The inquiry was tinged with disbelief.

'A light trim.'

Mr Tozer smirked dutifully and tucked a roll of cotton wool between Pumphrey's neck and collar. 'Nice weather you've brought, sir.'

Pumphrey slipped the platitude beneath his mental spectroscope. 'Brought' lit up on the reading scale. He had been recognized and challenged as a newcomer to the town.

'Yes, isn't it.'

A gentle touch guided his head slightly to one side. Covertly he held his view of Tozer's face in the mirror. It was a dark and knobbly face, very long so that the chin rested on the shirt front and was flanked by the lapels of the white coat. The ears were as long as bacon rashers and had pendulous, furry lobes. So deeply had the eyes retired within their sockets that they seemed to belong to a hermit crab peering warily from the refuge of Mr Tozer's skull.

'Just passing through, sir?' The barber's hand reached far out over Pumphrey and hovered uncertainly over the range of instruments behind the wash-basin. It seemed about to descend upon a bone-handled razor.

Pumphrey watched the razor. 'That is so,' he said. The hand moved on and picked up a pair of clippers.

'A short holiday, perhaps. No, but you're not a fisherman, I reckon.'

'Not exactly,' said Pumphrey. He realised he was quite without means of determining whether Tozer's feelers were threatening or conciliatory. The Hopjoy dossier had been indeterminate on all points except the fact that investigation and maintenance of contact with this man (to what end was not stated) had involved expense to date of £248 15s. Pumphrey thought quickly about this and found it encouraging. Tozer, on whatever side he was ranged, clearly had his price. He was unlikely to be really dangerous while the bidding was open.

'I thought,' said Pumphrey, 'that I might run across a friend of mine. I've an idea he came here to live a year or two back.'

'Nice to meet old friends. Oh, to meet old friends *is* nice.' Mr Tozer, mowing an ice-cold path up Pumphrey's neck, seemed grateful that an acceptable course of conversation had been signalled. He noisily blew the gathering of black fluff from the clipper blades and readjusted the angle of Pumphrey's head. 'There's only one thing nicer,' he resumed, 'and that's making new friends. And if there's one thing nicer than that, why, it's making friends *for* your friends. Now me ...' he applied to Pumphrey's neck a cloud of talcum powder from what looked like an old omnibus hooter – 'me, I'm what you might call a friend-*gatherer*. I was born ugly, you see, sir, and I accept it. No use fighting against your own nature. No use expecting other people to love you. Some of us are lovable; some aren't. It's like being musical. Put me at the piano and I couldn't play a note to save my life. Yet I love music; I'll listen to it for hours. Friendship, now: it's not for me. I know that. But it's something I like to know is going on all around. I enjoy it from a distance, like church bells. Funny, that, isn't it? And so do you know what I do? I foster it, I fertilise it. In any way I can, I help it along. You might say that bringing people together is my little private mission in life. And what, sir' – he turned and blew another fluff crop from the clippers – 'did you say the name of this friend of yours is?'

Here, obviously, was a critical point. Tozer's discharge of windy idealism, tedious and meaningless in itself, had been a calculated prelude to challenge. The name of his friend ... the question had been delivered at the tail of a diversionary gust of sentimentality, as a gipsy fiddler might casually drop a vital message with the final flourish of his czardas.

Pumphrey made up his mind. As the barber lightly leaned spread fingers upon his cranium while reaching for a pair of scissors, he gave the only answer that would take the game forward. 'Hopjoy,' he murmured.

For a moment Mr Tozer remained quite still. Pumphrey tried to see in the mirror what reaction his face betrayed, but the barber's fingers had tensed and would allow no upward movement of his customer's head.

Then Mr Tozer relaxed and wheeled to the side of the chair. He beamed down on Pumphrey and performed a little arabesque of mid-air snipping with the scissors. 'Mr Hopjoy!' he repeated, with every appearance of finding the name enormously to his liking. 'One of my most regular gentlemen. I know him well. Very well. As a matter of fact, when you came in I was just wondering if he'd turn up this afternoon. It must be several days now since … But fancy you being a friend of Mr Hopjoy!'

Mr Tozer stepped back behind Pumphrey and began making small swoops with the scissors over the unprofitable scalp. He was still smiling. But above the smile, Pumphrey noticed in the mirror, was a frown.

'What I was saying just now about friendship …' Mr Tozer resumed. 'Mr Hopjoy's a great one for friends. He comes in here perhaps three times a week. To be groomed, if I might put it that way. It's nice to find a man nowadays who's particular as to grooming. "George," he'll say, "I'm meeting a friend tonight," and he'll wink and I'll spruce him up like a show dog and off he'll trot with a joke about the account … oh, you might tell him I've been asking kindly after him, by the way, sir … and then later on I fall to thinking of him with his friend, and you know it's rather nice to get that feeling of having played a part and helped things along and made sure there'd be no harm done.'

'No harm done?' echoed Pumphrey. 'But how could harm be done between friends?'

Mr Tozer released a jowl-flapping laugh. 'Easiest thing in the world, sir. But I see you've not quite taken my meaning, not caught on, so to speak ...' The sudden opening of the shop door set off the tiny alarum of its bell. Mr Tozer looked over his shoulder, excused himself, and joined the man who had summoned him with a conspiratorial nod from the doorway.

Pumphrey could distinguish no word of the brief, murmured conversation. When next Tozer came into his field of vision it was to stoop before a narrow cupboard. Pumphrey saw him extract a small square envelope, which he concealed in his hand before walking back to the door. There was another subdued exchange, part of which seemed jocular in character, and the door closed.

The whole transaction, whatever it was, had taken no more than a minute.

The barber, awkwardly pulling up his white coat so as to be able to reach his hip pocket, was again at Pumphrey's side. 'Anything on, sir? Spray ... cream ...'

'No, nothing.'

Mr Tozer repossessed himself of the scissors, which he poised over Pumphrey's face. 'The nostrils, now?' he inquired eagerly.

'Certainly not.'

'Ah, you're very wise, sir; clipping does tend to stimulate. I personally find the best answer to what we might vulgarly call the hairy nose-hole is to fire it a couple of times a year.' His eyes wandered to a jar stacked with wax tapers. 'Like a railway embankment, you know.'

Pumphrey shook his head vigorously. He had been staring at the cupboard. Was it the curious traffic in envelopes which had first attracted Hopjoy's attention? Here, no doubt, was some sort of relay station in the complicated intelligence system he had been trying to delineate. Had his too persistent patronage of Mr Tozer's shop aroused suspicion and ultimately brought to his lodgings the silent, workmanlike attendance of a liquidation cadre?'

'Would Mr Hopjoy's friends be your friends, by any chance, sir?' Mr Tozer was drawing out the cotton wool roll and assiduously brushing his collar.

'I suppose we might have one or two mutual acquaintances. Why?' Pumphrey spoke, refusing to be provoked by the calculatedly irritant quality of the barber's harping on friendship. He thought he recognised one of the newer East European techniques for drawing admission of political affiliations.

Mr Tozer winked. Or rather he drew down the blind at the end of one of his dark ocular tunnels. 'Ladies, I was thinking of in particular, sir. The best friends of all.'

What a lewd word was 'ladies', Pumphrey reflected. Then it dawned on him that the course of this man's chatter conformed remarkably closely to another, more familiar anti-counterespionage tactic. Its aim was the discrediting and incapacitation of the investigator by imputation of immoral motives and even actual involvement in compromising situations.

'I cannot imagine,' he said coldly, 'that my social life could be of the slightest concern to you.'

Mr Tozer shrugged and tweaked away the sheet. 'Just as you like, sir.' He did not sound offended and his smile lingered as he bent to brush the front of Pumphrey's coat. 'I try to be of service in these matters, that's all, as I'm sure …' – he stood upright and directed upon Pumphrey a full and friendly gaze – '… your old friend Mr Hopjoy will tell you.'

Chapter Seven

'I REALLY CAN'T see that you have any need to be worried about Bry. He's a bit of a rolling stone, you know.'

Gordon Periam certainly did not look anxious. His expression, which Purbright felt was probably habitual, was one of bland earnestness. The smooth face, rounded by a well-fleshed chin a couple of sizes too big, betokened placidity born of a sheltered existence. The mouth was calm, but set in the permanent pout of the protractedly unweaned. Even the little lobeless ears were suggestive, somehow, of infancy.

The inspector looked away from Periam's brown eyes, gentle and unblinking, and watched an arrowhead of duck winging out over the flats. The two men were seated on a bench at the side of the sea bank road that ran between the Neptune and the dunes, Purbright having declined the hotel manager's offer of his own littered and airless cloister in favour of what the policeman had sanguinely termed 'a blow along the front'.

In fact, there proved to be no wind at all, while 'front' was scarcely an accurate designation for a rampart some two miles from the nearest wave. But at least the smell of the sea was there: a cool yet pungent compound of weed and salted mud, threading through the scents of hot sand and yellowing dune grass.

'And surely,' Periam was saying, 'somebody has to be reported missing – officially, you know – before you chaps start looking into things. Who would report Bry missing?' The voice was level, untroubled, like that of an inquirer into natural history.

'Some of the neighbours are a little apprehensive, I believe. And there are one or two rather odd circumstances that we do feel need explaining.' Purbright's gaze was now upon a steamer smudging almost imperceptibly the grey-green rim of the horizon. 'You see, sir, we've taken the liberty of looking inside your house.'

'But ... but why? I can't understand this, inspector. Really I can't.' The slightest frown of reproof clouded Periam's brow.

Purbright sighed, as if acknowledging the distasteful and inconvenient nature of his investigation. 'When,' he asked, 'did you last see Mr Hopjoy?'

Periam considered. 'It was one night last week; wait a minute ... yes, Thursday night.'

'And where was this?'

'Oh, at home.'

'That would be before your marriage.'

'The day before, actually. Doreen and I were married on the Friday.'

'I see. Now tell me about Thursday, will you? You said you saw Mr Hopjoy that evening. Were you not together earlier?'

'No, he hadn't got up by the time I left the house. I drove over here after breakfast and brought some things – mine and Doreen's. The room had been booked and I'd arranged to move in the day before the wedding so that everything would be ready. Well, that's just what I did. Once the stuff had been shifted out of the car I just killed time toddling around and having meals. Then I went to bed. It was quite early: about nine, I should say. I'd just nicely dropped off when the phone rang – there's one by the bed, you know.'

'It was rather a queer call, really, now that I come to think, but I was a bit muzzy, being wakened like that, and I didn't ask the girl's name. She just said she was speaking for Bry and would I come over right away. Then she rang off. Well, what could I do? I dressed and drove back to Flaxborough.

'Bry was at home on his own. Naturally, I'd thought there'd be something wrong, but there wasn't. He just said he wanted to ask me a few things – oh, I can't even remember them: they weren't important. Strictly *entre nous* I got the impression he was a weeny bit tiddly. If it had been anyone else it would have got my rag out, but it's never any good getting waxy with Bry, it's like water off a duck's back. In any case, he'd been very decent about letting us have the car.

'To cut a long story short, I made allowances for his having imbibed not wisely but too well and humoured him. But I certainly lost some beauty sleep that night. Dor must have thought I'd been out on the tiles when I turned up at the registry office. No, you mustn't take that seriously – Dor's terribly sweet and … and loyal.'

Periam wound up his speech by taking from his pocket a paper bag which he offered to Purbright. The inspector declined graciously and resumed his contemplation of the horizon. He wondered if the production of the sweets had been a reflex comment on the bride.

'What is your general opinion of your neighbours, Mr Periam? In Beatrice Avenue, you know, and round about.'

Periam carefully unwrapped a toffee. 'Quite decent old sticks, mostly. I don't have much to do with them now that Mother's passed on.'

'Is there anyone among them who might have a grudge against you, do you think?'

'I'm sure there's not. Why?' Periam chewed very slowly and deliberately. The action gave his cheeks a melancholy elongation. Moose, thought Purbright.

'The fact is that we have received an anonymous letter. I don't see why you shouldn't know about it. It hints that you and Mr Hopjoy were having a row on that Thursday night, a violent row.'

'That's absolutely untrue, inspector. I told you I was a bit tetchy at being brought over for nothing, but I don't think I let it show. There certainly wasn't a tiff, or anything like that.'

'You arrived and later went off again in Mr Hopjoy's car?'

'The Armstrong, yes.'

'Which he had lent you for the wedding and the holiday following.'

'That's right. For our honeymoon.' Periam rummaged in his bag, drew out a toffee in green paper, then dropped it back in favour of one wrapped in pink.

'Where did you leave the car while you were in the house?'

'I put it in the garage.'

'So you'd expected to stay a while – long enough to make it worth putting the car away?'

'No, I hadn't, actually. But Bry doesn't like the car left on the street even for a few minutes. Whenever I borrow it I automatically take it right into the garage afterwards.' The double operation of talking and chewing seemed at this point to imperil Periam's retention of saliva. He sucked noisily and clapped a knuckle to his lips. 'Pardon me: wind in the willows.'

'Mr Hopjoy knew about your marriage, I suppose?'

'Of course.'

'He didn't attend, though?'

Periam shook his head. 'Very much the bachelor gay is Bry. He said if I insisted on meeting my doom, he wasn't going to be an accessory. That's the way he talks, you know – very dry.'

There was a pause. Frowning, Periam twisted a toffee paper into a tight spill. 'Look, I don't quite get this anonymous letter business … What's supposed to have been going on?'

Purbright looked at him steadily. 'Simply this, Mr Periam. We think that Mr Hopjoy might have come to some harm. In your house.'

The chewing ceased. 'Harm? What sort of harm?'

'Murder, actually.'

In Periam's face there came no change whatever. Purbright began to doubt if he had caught the final quiet reply. Then he saw movement of the pale, plump mouth. 'Oh, my God …' The words emerged like those of a man praying through the stricture of a noose. 'But this is dreadful … I … Look here, you mean you've …'

'We've not found the body, sir, no. I don't imagine we shall now.'

Periam's hand passed uncertainly across his forehead, as if exploring a wound. 'You'll really have to tell me what all this is about, inspector. Maybe you think I'm being a bit of a stupid-sides, but honestly to God I've not the faintest notion of what you're hinting at. Why should you think something's happened to Bry?'

'Can you,' Purbright countered, 'tell me where Mr Hopjoy can be found?'

'I could suggest lots of places, I suppose. He moves around a good deal. I told you that.'

'Without his car?'

'Well, there are trains, buses.'

'You suggest a fairly extended journey, then?'

'He certainly knew Dor and I were getting spliced and would be away for a while. There's no reason why he shouldn't have decided to take a holiday himself.'

'He didn't notify his employers, sir. They're just as anxious as anyone.'

'His employers?'

'You don't know who his employers are, Mr Periam?'

Periam looked away. 'I'm not sure what I ought to say to that one. I do have a fair idea, actually. Well, with Bry and Mother and me being rather special pals, things did come out, you know.'

'That's understandable.'

Periam brightened. 'It's gone no further, of course.' He looked again directly at Purbright. 'I suppose you chaps were genned up all along?'

'The police were given such information as Mr Hopjoy's employers thought desirable.'

'Well, then,' said Periam eagerly, 'you can see why old Bry should nip off without a by-your-leave every now and again. Sometimes those fellows are away for years and their own wives don't know where they've gone.'

'How long were Mr Hopjoy's absences as a rule, sir?'

'Not terribly long, actually. He's quite often away for the night, though. Sometimes two or three in a row.'

'And you're never anxious on that account?'

'Not really. It's a bit of a nuisance sometimes, not knowing whether to lock up or not. But after all, what he's doing is fearfully necessary – I mean we'd be properly in the soup if the job weren't done by somebody.'

'A little while ago you said you thought Mr Hopjoy had been drinking when you went back to the house last Thursday night. Was he in the habit of drinking – drinking fairly heavily, I mean?'

'That's not easy to say, inspector. You see although we're pretty chummy when we're both at home we scarcely ever go around together outside, so I can't swear he goes into pubs or anything like that.'

'You wouldn't be surprised if he did, would you, Mr Periam? It's a fairly normal recreation.'

Periam smiled sadly. 'You wouldn't have persuaded Mother to think so. I don't mean she wasn't a good sport; it was just that she had a horror of sozzling. It's funny she never twigged that Bry was a bit squiffy sometimes.'

Absently, Periam felt in the bag he still clutched, withdrew a toffee and began unwrapping it. Then, changing his mind, he twisted the paper tight again. He looked up to see Purbright watching him. 'Mustn't spoil my lunch. As a matter of fact I really ought to be getting back.'

He stood and looked expectantly at Purbright. The policeman made no immediate move. Then he shook his head. 'You know, Mr Periam, this won't do, will it?'

Periam slowly lowered himself to sit on the edge of the bench, half turned towards Purbright. 'How do you mean? What won't do?'

'Five minutes ago you were a good deal shocked at the suggestion that your friend had been murdered. Now you're anxious not to spoil your lunch.'

Periam drew breath to reply, hesitated, then said quietly: 'No, it was Dor I was thinking of; she'll be wondering where

I am. Of course I'm upset. Terribly. I'm just one of those people who don't always show their feelings. In any case, you still haven't told me what's supposed to have happened.'

'That, Mr Periam, is because I don't think you told the truth about your return home last Thursday night.'

Periam looked down. 'I was fibbing a bit, as a matter of fact.'

'Why?'

'It was before you said anything about ... you know, about Bry. I didn't want Doreen's name to be dragged into it. The shindy was to do with her, you see.'

'There was a row, then?'

'Well ... yes, I'm afraid there was. A sort of row, anyway.' Periam's face muscles tightened. 'It was quite one-sided. Bry bawled me out, if you must know. I suppose I deserved it, but he certainly gave me old Harry. What I said about his having had one or two was quite right, by the way – I should think he'd been getting up some Dutch courage to have things out with me.'

Purbright watched Periam's hands. Tightly clasped, they were being pushed into the flesh of his thighs in a kind of kneading self-punishment.

'The truth is,' Periam went on, 'that Doreen was Bry's fiancée. They'd been going together for quite a while. He brought her home to tea once or twice when Mother was still alive. Then she started coming more often – after we lost Mother, I mean. She insisted on having a key and popping in to make things shipshape two or three times a week. She did most of the shopping and got us quite a few meals. Dor really is a brick, you know.

'Anyway, as time went on it just happened that we saw rather a lot of each other. You see, I was home more than Bry and … well, that's how it was. It sounds terribly disloyal, but I mean when two people find they're meant for each other … Of course, we didn't do anything … well, you know – nothing like that. It was rather awful, all the same, having to face old Bry day after day knowing I'd let him down. I simply couldn't tell him. Nor could Doreen; she hadn't the heart, poor kid. So we decided to slip off and get married and face the music afterwards. It sounds a rotten thing to do, but … oh, I don't know …' Periam lapsed into silence.

'It isn't true, then,' said Purbright, 'that Hopjoy lent you his car for your honeymoon. Nor that you told him you were getting married, for that matter.'

'No, I suppose it isn't. Actually I said I was having a holiday on my own. That's what I told Joan, too – Miss Peters at the shop.'

'Then have you any idea how Mr Hopjoy knew where to telephone you last Thursday night? And how he knew – as presumably he did – that you were about to get married?'

'It wasn't he who phoned, remember. I didn't recognise the voice of the girl who did, but my guess is that she was a friend of Bry's who had heard what was going on from someone Doreen had confided in. Dor's terribly sweet, but she does tend to let her heart rule her head. I tell her sometimes that she's much too trusting.'

Purbright seemed to accept the explanation. 'I should like,' he said, 'to hear a little more about this quarrel you now say took place between you and Hopjoy. Was there any violence – actual physical violence, I mean?'

'Oh, no; no fisticuffs or anything like that. He just … well, ranted. At the top of his voice. I don't know whether any of the neighbours heard. It's a pretty solidly built house, fortunately, so I can only hope they were asleep.'

'Were you in any particular part of the house?'

Periam made a sound distantly related to a laugh. 'It was in the bathroom of all places. Bry called me up when he heard me come in. He'd been having a wash, I expect.'

'And he …?'

'Let off at me. He seemed to be trying to get my goat. Of course I can't complain – I had pinched his young lady, after all – but he did come it a bit strong.'

Periam consulted a watch that he drew from his trousers pocket after first removing a leather purse. 'Look here, I really must see to the inner man. It's just on one.'

'It is, indeed. Perhaps I ought to see to my inner man, too.' Purbright rose, a little stiffly. 'If you think I might be introduced to Mrs Periam without causing her too much alarm …'

'Well, I … I'm not sure that …'

'I'm sorry, sir. I assure you I don't make a habit of intruding on honeymoons. There are some more things I must ask you, though – both of you – and they might as well be put socially, especially as everyone seems to be hungry.'

Together they set off towards the Neptune, Periam silent and staring gloomily aside from time to time at the lavender-coloured marsh with its silver fringe of distant sea, and Purbright preoccupied with the compatibility or otherwise of murder by acid bath with a world of chums, young ladies, and the Student Prince.

Neither looked remotely expectant of enjoyment. It was natural for the few people they passed on the way back to the hotel to assume, if they noticed them at all, that they were holiday-makers.

Chapter Eight

Hopjoy's reports upon the old Moorish Electric Theatre, Flaxborough, had been suggestive, espionage-wise, to an encouraging degree. Ross, having savoured their subtlety and noted how much their compilation had cost in expenses, felt that a personal follow-up should be undertaken without delay.

He parked the Bentley where it would be unobtrusive among a score of farmers' cars against the northern pavement of the Corn Exchange. Immediately opposite was the flaking, ochred façade of the old theatre. The general idea of its columns and arches, its filigree screens, and onion dome, had been the simulation of oriental splendour, but the fabric now looked diseased and pulpy. Within an arched opening beneath the dome once had stood, each Monday and Thursday, a junior commissionaire embarrassingly victimised by the whims of a zealous manager; robed and turbaned, wool-whiskered, and smeared with shoe polish, this miserable sham muezzin had called forth the film titles and programme times to the faithful beneath. Now a mound of pigeon droppings almost filled the enclosure and a few tatters of faded paper flapped from the column-supported billboard, four-year-old relics of the cinema's last dying week.

The main arch, which had spanned the entrance doors and paybox, was boarded up, but this drab barricade was pierced with a small door surmounted with the words: 'Alhambra Club – Licensed for Billiards'.

Ross's attention turned to a figure on the steps near the door. It was a one-legged man, who gave a first impression of being all chest and crutch. Then, jammed into the great blue-jerseyed barrel, a face became discernible. It was of the colour of smoked bacon rind and traversed with even darker lines, the concertina creases of immoderate mirth. The nose was a knobbled crudity, approximately central and perforated by pores suggestive of the inflictions of a shotgun. The mouth was a leathern slit, the eyes shiny black beetles that scuttled in perpetual restlessness back and forth along deep crevices.

The man wore a tiny black waterproof peaked cap, tugged down over one ear. Slung from his shoulders was a tray of paper flags, each bearing the image of a sick terrier looking through a lifebelt. The poster hanging from the tray invited contributions to the Dogs at Sea Society.

If the man was a parody of the Ancient Mariner, his solicitations were a good deal more forceful than those of an original contented merely with stopping one of three. With the air of one brandishing a blunderbuss, he thrust a collecting tin beneath the nose of every citizen who had neglected to cross to the other side of the street.

Ross watched the brisk and successful exactions for some minutes, at first idly, then with sharpened interest. He noticed that an occasional alms-giver failed in some small way to conform to the general pattern. These exceptions fumbled their gifts, but not in the normal manner of pretending a halfpenny to be a florin; they actually pushed paper, not coins, into the tin.

Bank notes? Surely, Ross reasoned, not even from the besotted ranks of dog-lovers would this villainous old sailorman manage to extort so extravagant a tribute. And those who produced the folded slips of paper certainly did not look wealthy.

There came a spell when the stream of passers-by slackened. The one-legged man hitched up his jersey, consulted a watch extracted from the region of his stomach, peered up and down the street and wheeled on his crutch to face the small door. With a sudden lurch he barged it open and disappeared.

Ross left the car and walked up the steps.

Closing the club door behind him, he stood listening and adjusting his eyes to the gloom of what had been the foyer of the Moorish Electric. The only illumination came from a grime-encrusted bulb, fashioned like a flame, that sprouted from a torch held aloft by a gilded plaster slave-girl. Ross fleetingly felt old memories stir at the sight of the statue's ingenious mutilations, unhurriedly executed, he supposed, by cruel young men with enormous snooker handicaps.

The air carried a ghost of disinfectant perfume and aisle carpeting but it was heavily overlaid with the brackish smell of damp masonry. Two ascending staircases at right and left, only the first few steps of which could be discerned in what little light reached them, had been blocked off with crossed planks. Flakes of tarnished gilt lay on the bare floor, but whatever mock-Moorish conceits had shed them mouldered invisible in the upper darkness.

Ross saw at once which way the flag-seller had passed. One of a pair of cut glass and mahogany doors still swung gently beneath the sign 'Stalls'. He pushed his way through them to the gently inclined corridor beyond. Two similar doors, admitting a greenish twilight, were at the further end. He walked to them and peered cautiously through the glass.

What had been the ground floor of the cinema was now stripped of seats. Ross saw rows of dark slabs, each surmounted with its pyramidal cowling, stretching away into the gloom. Only the three nearest billiard tables were in use. Scattered snooker balls shone like multi-coloured globular flowers on their bright baize lawns. Here and there a face blossomed yellowly among them, squinting along a cue.

Watchers of the play – Ross guessed their number to be about two dozen – were invested with a sinister anonymity: the light from the tables fell only upon their trunks and arms. When comments were made, and they were terse and infrequent, it was quite impossible to judge who had spoken.

Ross squeezed into the hall and moved to one side of the doorway. His arrival, if it had been heeded, went unchallenged. Looking to his left, he saw that a long counter had been built against perhaps half the length of the rear wall. Two small shaded bulbs, in conformity with the general scheme of dimness, showed rows of cues, a clock and a table-booking board. Standing behind the counter was a man with thin, sandy hair who was scrutinising, apparently with difficulty, a newspaper that he had folded to the area of a prayer book.

Ross edged casually along the counter. When he was quite near, the man looked up sharply.

'You a member, sir?'

The question was unnecessarily loud. The headless spectators around the tables undulated slightly as if moved by a sudden current through the waist-deep darkness in which they stood. And Ross glimpsed, at the far end of the counter, another movement. The old sailorman, quick as a lizard, had taken off and replaced his jaunty cap.

Ignoring, for the moment, the steward, Ross gazed full at the flag-seller and was treated to a wink that threatened to expel the old man's eye like a black pip. Before Ross turned away, he had seen that the collecting tin standing beside the tray of flags on the counter now lacked its slotted lid.

'A member of the club? No, I'm not, as it happens.'

'If you're looking for someone, perhaps I could …' The steward's voice had resumed normal pitch.

Ross looked back over his shoulder. 'I don't think he's here at the moment. The light's not terribly good, though.' He stole another glance at the sailorman. The top was back on his tin.

'Well, tell me his name; you've only to tell me his name.' The voice was tired, querulous. Small fry, thought Ross: the easily exasperated are never allowed deeply in. He said: 'There's nothing against my hanging on for a bit, is there?'

The steward looked dubious. Ross felt that he wanted to consult with a look the one-legged man but dared not. Finally he shrugged and returned to his newspaper. 'Just as you like …'

The atmosphere in the hall, though cold and stale, had something of a soporific quality, deepened by the gentle rumble of the balls and the constant clicks of impact. Ross, his eyes half closed, drowsily contemplated the silent perambulation of the players and amused himself by judging from isolated jackets and ties and hands the characters of the faceless watchers. Among them were a few, a couple, one only perhaps, of the painfully, carefully cultivated contacts of Hopjoy, little studs of sensitivity along the line of F.7. But which? And by what sign would he divine them?

'P'raps you fancy a game, sir?'

Beside him was the bellows face of the mariner. The old man bore a smell compounded of raspberry jam and oil stove.

'A game?' Ross had been unprepared for an approach quite in this manner. 'I'm not a member, you know.'

The other waved a hand disdainfully. 'What's that matter?' It sounded like 'wozzard-madder'. Twelve miles south-west of King's Lynn, calculated Ross. He took his hand from his pocket. 'All right, then.'

The Norfolkman gave two light taps with his crutch against the counter. Without looking up, the steward reached behind him and flicked a switch. 'Number five,' he muttered. 'There's a set on.'

Ross reached across the counter and selected a cue from the rack. The steward offered him no assistance but instead, still without taking his eyes from his paper, stooped for a black japanned cue case evidently kept in custody for the sailor's personal use.

'I can't play, mind,' asserted Ross's opponent, unlocking his case and withdrawing the cue with the relish of a fencing master challenged by a splenetic woodcutter.

'In that case,' said Ross, 'we'll just play for the table, shall we?'

The sailorman looked shocked. 'Oh, I don't say I mind losing a little. Just to make it interesting.'

'A pound?' Ross sounded as though injecting interest into the encounter were beyond his power or concern. 'Five? Anything you like – within reason, you know.' He bent and blew a flake of ash from the cloth.

'A quid, then. I'm not much to beat. I told you.'

Ross smiled inwardly at the man's predictable mendacity. He would prove, undoubtedly, formidable by small town poolroom standards. But mere shilling-catching competence was of no avail against the expertise acquired at a guinea a point in the basement of Harding's in Rangoon, or at Billiards-Bec, behind Rue-des-Ecoles, where Charpentier had had the slate beds of his tables faced with leaves of topaz.

The sailorman spun a coin. Ross called.

'You can break, matey.' Ross had not been shown the coin, but he obediently took sight and sent the cue ball with enough spin to rebound from the end cushion, kiss the corner of the triangle of reds, and roll, via two more cushions, snugly behind the brown.

'Ah, very crafty,' said the sailorman. 'I reckon this is where I give some away.' He handed Ross his crutch, hopped with astonishing agility round the table, and propped himself into position to take a quick, powerful, and apparently aimless stroke. The white rocketed to one cushion after another, missing everything on the board until it finally crashed into the group of red balls, which disintegrated like a poppy in a gale.

'By God, that was a fluke, matey. I do believe one's gone down.'

'Three, to be exact,' corrected Ross.

'Three? You don't say!' He leered at the scattered spheres, then sighed. 'That's my lot, though; there's not a colour that'll go.' Off-handedly he nominated black, made his stroke, and looked away. The cue ball hit the black fully, then curled back and came to rest tight in a pocket angle. The blue lay between it and the only accessible red.

Ross handed back the crutch. Almost kneeling, he introduced the tip of his cue through the mesh of the pocket net and delivered a sharp upward stroke. The white rose six inches into the air, sailed over the blue and struck in turn four reds, the last of which cannoned off yellow and trickled into a centre pocket.

'I reckon you've played before, matey.' The compliment was tinged with anxiety. Several watchers at the next table turned and shuffled nearer.

Ross smoothly sank the black, another red, black again. A third red lay an inch from the pocket mouth. The cue snaked forward a fraction left of centre of the white ball to impart side. Incredibly, it slid off and veered to one side with a rattle; the white rolled foolishly into impact with the pink.

'Oh, hard cheese! Bloody hard cheese, matey!'

Acknowledging this jubilant condolence with a shrug, Ross glanced at the tip of his cue. There glistened upon it a few tiny bubbles of saliva.

The sailorman, propelled around the table by the noiseless spring of his single leg, wielded his cue like a compensatory natural limb. With every stroke, the swiftly changing pattern of brightly coloured orbs was diminished.

As Ross watched the great bounding barrel, he sensed the satisfaction of the silent audience, one of whose fingers, deftly spittled, had stolen from the dark to cut short his own success. He was no more resentful of that malicious intervention than he would have been of the secretion of a bomb in his car boot. 'Unfair', Ross knew perfectly well, was a word with meaning only for cowards and failures. The game, of course, was lost, but winning or losing in so trivial a context concerned him not at all. His attention was riveted upon a point just behind his preoccupied opponent's right ear (that point, by quaint coincidence, at which a firmly driven ice pick or bradawl would reliably produce immediate loss of consciousness and rapid death).

Protruding beneath the greasy band of the man's cap was the corner of a slip of paper.

Ross wasted no time speculating on whether the paper could be surreptitiously tweaked away, even in a moment of contrived confusion. It would have to be snatched audaciously and run off with. And luck would be needed: most of the score or so of taciturn onlookers were unquestionably the man's allies. The fact that he could not see their faces gave him no hope of their being pacific or infirm.

There remained only blue, pink, and black upon the board. The sailorman hoisted his trunk on the table's edge and drew back the butt of his cue. Ross moved closer behind him. The white ball flew to the blue, despatched it slickly into an end pocket and rolled obediently back to within three inches of the cushion. The sailorman grunted, levered himself upright and took a rearward hop.

Before he could bend to take aim at the pink, there flashed to his neck the hand of Ross, who was already half-turned for flight.

With a bellow the one-legged man dropped his cue and grasped the back of his head as if stung by a wasp. Ross already was three strides nearer the swing doors, bearing with him the man's crutch.

Escape seemed open. Ross plunged for the doors. Then, unaccountably, his legs scissored upon something hard and slim. He spun helplessly off course and crashed to the floor, pain ballooning in his thigh.

In the darkness, a man drew back his cue and assured himself it was unbroken. Then he stooped quickly and picked up the crutch.

Ross rolled under the nearest table to recover his breath. He glanced at the doors. Half a dozen heads were silhouetted against the glass. There would, though, be emergency exits. He thrust the captured piece of paper into his cigarette case and crawled out into the gangway.

The sailorman, his incredible mobility restored, was stumping to and fro near the spot where Ross had been brought down. After a while, he began to move from table to table, systematically, feeling for his quarry with sweeps and jabs of his crutch. Ross, bending low, crept away from the sound of his exploratory advance. He wondered how long it would be before the steward, by now doubtless assigned some part in the hunt, switched on all the lights.

Or was the persistent gloom an agreed precaution against identification?

Apparently not. There was a click, followed by another and another. Soon the bulbs over every table were blazing.

Ross lay flat. He was now nearly in the middle of the hall, in one of the patches of shadow immediately beneath the tables themselves that were still deep enough to give him concealment.

He looked quickly around. The legs of the hunters in the gangways were plainly visible. They moved without haste. Now and then a pair of legs bent and the outline of an inverted head descended. Unexcited murmurs and mutterings reached him.

Above them, a voice rose loud. 'Come on, matey. Stand up and stop playing silly buggers. Nobody's going to hurt you.'

Ross snaked across to the shelter of the next table. He had spotted a red painted door in the centre of the nearer wall. If he could cross three more gangways, he would reach it.

'I want to talk to you. Stop farting about, damn you.' The probing crutch crashed against a table leg. Ross made another shuffling sortie on hands and knees. He gained five more yards.

For some seconds, the place was absolutely silent. Then he heard a curious trundling sound. It quickly grew louder, diminished with the same rapidity, and ended in a distant crash.

Again it was quiet. Then the noise was repeated. This time it seemed louder, nearer. Ross tried to interpret it, but in vain. Once more the swift, menacing rumble passed through the hall, climaxed with a great hammer blow.

At the instant the noise began for the fourth time, Ross realised what was happening. His adversary was trying to bowl him out of hiding – or, more likely, incapacitate him – with one of the heavy, flint-hard snooker balls that he was sending in vicious under-arm volleys along the floor.

This fourth missile, Ross knew with certainty, was bound straight for its target. He knew too that the tiny fraction of time that remained before its violent arrival would permit of not the slightest self-protective movement. The immediately impending pain could not be begged off. Embrace it, then, his brain commanded; lumpenly absorb the agony and store it as a fuel of retaliation.

In the path of the hurtling ball, Ross became limp as a new corpse. The incredibly effectual mental annealing processes of Course Five were now being proved. His mind was a calm, dark void, prepared for pain's fertilising penetration.

It did not come. Three feet short of Ross's head, the ball rose miraculously and shot past his ear.

Wonderingly, Ross reached out and groped for what had saved him. His fingers met an angular fragment. It was the vestige of a cube of billiard chalk.

The bowling went on methodically. But the particular danger it represented had passed with the diversion of the sailorman's attention to other rows of tables. Looking back along the floor, Ross saw that the followers of the attempt to drive him to a view were moving in a group behind the bowler. They seemed in general a good deal less anxious to mount an offensive than the earlier intervention of the man with the cue had suggested. Ross decided that his best course was open retreat, coupled with the risk of the red door's being locked.

He crawled swiftly across the last two aisles and rose to his feet, lifting the door's catch bar at the same time. He pushed. The door remained shut. A hoarse, angry cry signalled his having been seen. As he heaved against the unyielding door he heard the rapid thumping of the enemy crutch. He put his foot against the bar and kicked. This time the long-disused bolts jumped from their corroded sockets. The door swung back and Ross leaped into blinding daylight.

He was in a passage comfortingly filled with the noises of the street at its end. In a few seconds Ross stepped out into the Corn Exchange.

No one had followed him.

Chapter Nine

IN THE NEPTUNE kitchen, a waiter reached up through the warm, savoury steam and pulled a bottle of 1953 Beaune from the rack. He tossed it jocundly from hand to hand a few times, twirled it in the dust box, and cradled it. Just before he passed through the service doors into the restaurant, he stiffened his unexceptional face into the lineaments of omniscient superiority and drew back his shoulders. Then he glided to the table of Gordon Periam and party, bearing the wicker basket as if it contained the last surviving fragment of the True Cross.

Periam looked up. 'Ah.' He reached out and touched the bottle. 'Is it cold?'

The waiter winced. 'You did ask for a Beaune, sir. A *red* wine.' He drew back the basket and stared with pained incredulity at Periam's finger marks in the dust.

'You would wish me to decant it, sir?'

'You'd better, yes.'

Back in the kitchen, the waiter briskly uncorked the bottle between his knees and tumbled three parts of its contents, merrily gurgling, into a jug. The remainder, thriftily, he swigged.

While the waiter contrived, in comfortable wine-warmed scrutiny of the *Daily Mirror*, an interval suitable to the delicacy of his supposed task, Inspector Purbright took stock of Mrs Periam.

She would be, he estimated, twenty-six or twenty-seven years old, although an almost offensively inept hair style – plaits coiled into round pads over her ears – gave a first impression of mid-thirties. In the plump white face, brown eyes looked out with an alert directness which might have been adjudged a token of honesty; Purbright was not quite sure, though, whether their frankness was unalloyed with pleading, a hint of nymphomania. He resisted the suspicion partly because he felt it to be unfair at such short acquaintance, partly because of his awareness that the self-flattery of the middle-aged too often takes the form of a fancied discernment of sexual irresponsibility in younger women.

Nevertheless, a certain physical lushness about Doreen Periam was undeniable. It was rendered the more disturbing by the paradoxical prissiness of her dress. The frock she was wearing, for instance, was an outlandish affair in heavy, dark blue silk, that seemed to have been designed to constrict her bust into prudish formlessness. Its actual effect was to squeeze up into provocative cloven prominence at the base of her neck the breasts that a less 'modest' garment would have accommodated quite unspectacularly. From the long, tightly cuffed sleeves emerged small hands as white and delicate as potato shoots. Their continual movement might have been merely a symptom of genteel nervousness. But as they strayed over the dark silk, they seemed to be exploring underlying areas of erotic ache.

'I think we can acknowledge quite frankly between the three of us,' Purbright was saying, 'that until recently you were a particular friend of Mr Hopjoy, Mrs Periam.'

She glanced apprehensively at Periam, who nodded. 'I told the inspector about that, darl. He understands how things were.'

'It's just that he wasn't ... wasn't the right one. It does happen, you know.' The bright, brown eyes had widened.

'Of course. I'd like to know, though, whether he accepted that view. Was he reconciled to your preference having changed?'

'Oh, I'm sure he was, really. I mean a boy's bound to be upset when someone else comes along, but mostly it's his pride that's hurt. Don't you think so?'

Purbright declined to endorse the sentiment. He was wondering whether Doreen were as simple as she sounded. 'Jealousy, Mrs Periam, isn't altogether a matter of hurt pride. From what your husband has told me already, I'd say that Mr Hopjoy took the affair rather badly.'

'Our barney in the bathroom, darl,' interjected Periam. 'Remember I told you.'

'Oh, that ...' She looked down at the cloth and absently edged a fork from side to side. 'I suppose I was a bit of a beast to him, really. Brian was so happy-go-lucky, though; I never thought he'd come the old green-eyed monster.'

Periam took her hand. 'It was my fault. We should have broken it to him sooner.'

The waiter, priest-like, was at Periam's shoulder. He administered a sacramental sample, then straightened to stare gravely into the middle distance. Purbright was reminded of a well-bred dog owner awaiting the conclusion of his animal's defecation in a neighbour's gateway.

Periam sipped, assumed for some seconds the wine-man's look of trying to work out a square root in his head, then nodded reassuringly at his wife. 'I think you'll find it not too bad. Maybe a shade young ...' The waiter, who thought he had spotted the arrival of an expense account junta at the far side of his territory, hurriedly filled the three glasses and took himself off.

Doreen pronounced the Beaune 'nice but a bit acid'. Purbright glanced at Periam's face. It betrayed no sign of his having found the remark unfortunate.

The girl resumed her contemplation of the tablecloth. Her hand remained clasped in her husband's. After a while she disengaged it and, unconsciously, it seemed, allowed it to fall into Periam's lap. She smiled. 'Fancy,' she said, half to herself, 'you and old Brian having a set-to over poor little me.'

'Well, not a set-to, exactly,' Periam said. He captured Doreen's hand, which had been running affectionately up and down his thigh, and returned it to table level. 'It was Bry who flew off the handle. I couldn't get a word in edge-ways.'

The soup arrived. Both Periam and his bride hitched forward their chairs and looked pleased. Their honeymoon seemed to have given them an appetite.

'You did a certain amount of housekeeping at Beatrice Avenue, didn't you, Mrs Periam?'

'I popped in occasionally during the week. Since Gordon lost his mother, you know.'

'You cooked, and so forth?'

'That's right.'

'Tell me: did you have anything to do with the neighbours? You don't know of any who were especially inquisitive?'

The girl shook her head without interrupting the spooning of her soup.

'Did any friends of Mr Hopjoy ever visit the house?'

'Not while I was there.' She turned to Periam. 'I don't think he ever brought anyone home, did he, Gordon?'

'No, he was always a bit of a dark horse in that respect. Mind you ...' – he carefully piloted an undissolved pellet of soup powder to the rim of his plate – 'you have to remember the sort of job he does.'

'Do you know what Mr Hopjoy was doing, Mrs Periam?'

The plump shoulders rose slightly. 'I suppose I do really. In a way ...' Again her eyes consulted Periam's. 'I don't want to get him into trouble or anything ...'

'I fancy that possibility no longer exists,' Purbright said quietly.

Doreen looked mildly puzzled. 'Because you think he's skipped off, you mean? Oh, but he often does that. That's why he told me just a little bit about his job; he didn't want me to imagine The Worst, as they say.' There was a flash of tiny, very white teeth. The smile faded slowly; the girl seemed to sustain it deliberately in order to warm the image her words had created.

'Did he tell you where he went, or anything about the people he met?'

'Well, he didn't actually mention places or names. He'd just say something about having to meet a contact, or what he called "one of our people". Then at night – all night, quite often – he kept a watch on houses of people he'd been tipped off about ... that's what he said, wasn't it, Gordon?'

Periam murmured: 'That's right, darl.' He appeared to be more interested in the next course, which was just then arriving. Purbright glanced without elation at the slices of denatured chicken, awash in suspiciously brown and copious gravy; then involuntarily drew back as the waiter performed manual pirouettes in the process of depositing upon his plate portions of dropsical potato and tinned peas.

'Everything to your satisfaction, madam?' Bending low over Doreen's shoulder, his face as stiff as a dead deacon's, the waiter delivered the question into the top of her dress. Echo-sounding, thought Purbright idly.

'I'm afraid,' the inspector said a little later, 'that I'm going to have to deprive you of Mr Hopjoy's car.'

The honeymooners simultaneously stopped eating. 'Oh, no!' Doreen's fleshy little mouth tightened. 'That's not fair; Brian lent it to us specially.'

'I'm terribly sorry, but there it is. We'll not keep it longer than is absolutely necessary.'

'But what's the car to do with ... with all this?'

'Perhaps nothing, Mr Periam. It's just that policemen have no choice in the matter of leaving stones unturned.'

Doreen impatiently stabbed a piece of chicken. 'You won't find Brian in the boot, if that's what you're getting at.'

Purbright looked at her and sighed. 'You know, Mrs Periam, I hate to be solemn at meal times, but I feel it's only proper to tell you – as I told your husband this morning – that we are quite seriously concerned with the possibility that Mr Hopjoy's disappearance will prove permanent.'

The admonition produced no reaction beyond a quick little shake of the head. 'He'll turn up: don't you worry.' If this girl had been consciously party to a crime, Purbright reflected, it was clearly of no use hoping that she would be harrowed into acknowledging it.

*

When he arrived back at the police station, Purbright found his desk neatly stacked with Sergeant Love's gleanings from 14 Beatrice Avenue. He sought Love out.

'Righto, Sid: astound me.'

Love looked doubtfully at the pile of papers. 'I collected everything I could find. There's nothing very exciting, though.'

'Never mind. Let's have a look.'

The sergeant picked up the first few sheets. 'Letters to Periam. Either he didn't get many or he didn't keep them. There's nothing recent.'

Three of the letters appeared to be from female relatives. They offered condolence on the death of Periam's mother. 'She was a beautiful soul,' ran one, written in a wavery but florid hand, 'and I know that no one can ever take her place. But, Gordon dear, you must not let your grief be a door closed against all other affection. Dear Mackie – and I'm sure you won't mind me mentioning her at this time – has been so patient and loyal, and what could never be so long as your duty lay with your poor mother is now quite possible and right.' The signature was 'Auntie B'.

A fourth letter was from a solicitor and enumerated final details of the administration of Mrs Periam's will. The other two were formal acknowledgements of a transfer of deeds and a small quantity of stock.

'This,' said Love, handing over a second, thicker sheaf, 'is just shop stuff – you know, his tobacco business.'

Purbright glanced quickly through the invoices, delivery notes and receipts, and put them aside. Love picked up his next selection. 'Periam again. Certificates, documents, and all that.'

'You should have been an archivist, Sid.' The sergeant, suspecting an ironic indecency, grinned to show his broadness of mind.

The third batch of papers was unproductive of anything more exciting than a faded copy of Mrs Periam's marriage lines, her son's birth certificate, and, crispest and most blackly inked of all, that of her death. There were several bank statements, showing Periam's credit standing at around £2,500; a couple of insurance policies; National Health Insurance cards, one in the name of Joan Peters, the shop assistant; some rates receipts and a card of membership of the Flaxborough Chamber of Trade.

Finally in the Periam collection came a miscellany topped by two years' back numbers of *Healthy Living* and a number of pamphlets on muscle development 'in the privacy of your own bedroom'. There were some scrolls commemorative of Gordon Halcyon Periam's achievements as pupil and teacher in the Carlton Road Methodist Sunday School. A small album of photographs seemed a typical record of family life in back gardens and beach huts; Purbright noticed the consistent role of the young Periam to be that of a frowning, slightly agape custodian of his mother's arm. An exceptional snapshot, marred by faulty development, showed him at the age of fifteen or sixteen, looking defensively at the camera in the company of a fat girl pouting at an ice cream cornet. Even in this picture, however, a segment of face in the top left corner indicated the fond and watchful presence of the late Mrs Periam.

Love licked a finger. 'Now for Hopjoy,' he announced. 'I didn't have such a job rooting these out. They were all stuffed into this writing case thing. I found it under his bed.'

'By the way, what did you make of that big bedroom at the back; I can't imagine who uses it.'

Love shook his head. 'Nobody does. It was the old lady's.'

Purbright looked up from his examination of the writing case. 'But it's cluttered up with all manner of things. Shoes, gewgaws, medicine bottles, hair nets. I noticed the bed was still made up, too. A bit odd, isn't it?'

'I saw a film once,' said Love, his face brightening, 'where a bloke kept a room like that for years after his mother was supposed to have been buried. She was in the wardrobe, actually, all shrivelled and he used to plonk her down in a chair at teatime and talk to her. It turned out that ...'

'Did you take a peek into the wardrobe, Sid?'

Love looked a little ashamed of himself. 'I did, as a matter of fact. Just in the course of things. There were some dresses in it. And a sort of basket thing.'

'Basket thing?' Purbright frowned, suddenly interested.

'That's right.' The sergeant sketched in the air with his hands. 'I should think it was one of those old contraptions dressmakers used to use.'

'I'm quite sure you're wrong, Sid. Never mind for now, though. Let's see what Mr Hopjoy left us.'

The Hopjoy bequest was not calculated to bring much joy to beneficiaries. It consisted, almost exclusively, of bills and accompanying letters that ranged in tone from elaborate politeness to vulgar exasperation.

Purbright mentally awarded top marks to the essay contributed by the manager of the Neptune.

My dear Mr Hopjoy (it began expansively),

I need hardly tell you how delighted I was to re-new the acquaintance, in the person of your charm-ing wife, of a lady I had mistakenly supposed to have married into a family on the other side of the county. I cannot say what gave me that erroneous impression: the man is almost unknown to me, save by repute as a choleric and well-muscled individual. You will, I am sure, apologise to Mrs Hopjoy for whatever trace of bewilderment I may stupidly have shown on being introduced to her (or re-introduced, should I say?) May I take this opportunity also to congratulate you upon your new union. The former Mrs Hopjoy – if I might make so bold as to offer comment – seemed possessed of a disconcertingly changeable personali-ty; there were times when I had difficulty in persuad-ing myself that she was the same woman. Now that a more settled marital relationship seems happily in prospect, I may, no doubt, look forward to the sat-isfactory adjustment of the incidental matter of your account.

Yours ever to serve,
P. BARRACLOUGH

'Adjustment', it appeared, involved the sum of £268 14s. To an even larger debt a letter from Mr J. O'Conlon made regretful reference. In this case, social overtones were absent. Mr O'Conlon merely expressed the hope that his client would avoid trouble for all concerned (including, especially, himself) by sending along his cheque for £421 at any time convenient to him within the following forty-eight hours.

'Bookmaking,' Purbright observed to Sergeant Love, 'must be looking up. I wouldn't have thought Joe O'Conlon had enough padding to let anyone have that much credit.'

Turning to the next sheet, Purbright raised his brows in mild astonishment. 'George Tozer, gentlemen's hairdresser,' he read out. 'To goods, £11 15s. 4d. A remittance will oblige or I'm sorry no more of same can be supplied.'

Love puffed out his schoolboy-pink cheeks. 'A proper lad, that Hopjoy. And on tick, too ...'

'You feel that makes his excesses the more reprehensible?'

'I wouldn't know about that, but I reckon they don't call old Tozer the poor man's friend for nothing.'

'You're sure you're not confusing the merchant with his merchandise?' Purbright put the barber's reckoning aside and picked up a letter from the Happy Motoring Finance Company. 'Ah, the car ... I was wondering when we'd come to that.'

'In the matter of your outstanding instalments, which now amount to £242 16s.,' the letter ran, 'I am directed to refer to your personal letter to Sir Harry Palmer, in which you say that the nature of certain confidential work undertaken by you for HM Government requires you to foster a false appearance of impecuniosity. I regret that the Chairman must decline your invitation to seek confirmation of your position from the Minister of State, as this would be outside the scope of our Company practice. Accordingly, I must inform you that unless your instalment payments are brought up to date within fourteen days we shall be obliged to take appropriate action.'

Purbright regarded the letter in silence for a while. Then he looked quickly through the rest of the contents of the writing case. Beneath the bills lay an unsuggestive miscellany of theatre programmes, hotel and resort brochures, a London restaurant guide, a couple of wine and food lists, maps, a jeweller's catalogue and the maintenance booklet for the Armstrong. Then came a wad of blank, thin paper sheets of the kind Purbright had seen in the hands of Ross, and finally a cheap writing pad from which the top sheet or two had been torn.

Purbright flicked through the pages of the pad. They enclosed nothing. He leaned back, staring out of the window and gently tapping the pad against the edge of the desk.

'I don't know,' he said slowly, 'how Mr Hopjoy rated as a counter-espionage agent, but if he applied to his job only half the talent he showed for fornication and insolvency I'd say Russia's had it.'

Love glanced at the inspector a little dubiously.

'Oh, don't worry, Sid. The fellow obviously made no secret of what he was up to. He even traded on it. I don't see why we should behave like old ladies pretending they can't smell the drains. Which reminds me ... wasn't Warlock coming in today some time?'

'About four,' Love said. 'He sounded jolly bouncy over the phone.'

'He's probably run across some little titbit like a fingernail or a kidney. Incidentally, I don't see anything among this lot that gives colour to Hopjoy's pose as a commercial traveller.'

'That's all there was at the house. Perhaps he had an office somewhere.'

Purbright shook his head. 'None of the chemists in the town remembers his calling. No, I think he just couldn't

102

be bothered to keep up that part of it; who was to care, anyway?'

The sergeant watched in silence as Purbright closed and fastened the writing case and pushed it and Periam's belongings to the back of the desk. Then, 'It's funny, you know,' he said hesitantly, 'but what with one thing and another – all that money trouble and everything – you might almost say that getting done must have come to that bloke as a happy release.' He swallowed. 'If you see what I mean.'

There was no flippancy in Purbright's voice when he replied: 'I do see what you mean, Sid. I do indeed.'

Chapter Ten

SERGEANT WARLOCK BLOSSOMED into Purbright's office like the man from the Prudential. He carried a briefcase and a squat, black wooden box with a handle.

'Now then, squire.' The luggage was placed in precise symmetry on the desk top. Warlock's hands, thus released, flew into joyful union and vigorously rubbed each other. 'How's tricks?'

Purbright conceded that tricks were merely so-so.

His visitor, after taking two turns round the room, in order, Purbright supposed, to dissipate some of the momentum of his arrival, poised himself by the briefcase and flicked it open. He looked zestfully at the inspector. 'Nicest little job I've had in years. Absolutely fascinating ...' His glance went down to the papers he was drawing from the case. 'I hardly know where to begin.'

'By sitting down, perhaps?' suggested Purbright unhopefully. Warlock chuckled and seemed to grow two inches taller there and then. He spread pages of typescript on the desk and rapidly reviewed the underlined sub-headings.

'Ah, well; we might as well start with the bath, eh? You were quite right about that. It was melted paraffin wax that had been brushed over the chipped parts and the metal plug seating. There were still traces of it, although I'd say the whole caboodle had been sluiced out afterwards with water from the hot tap. And the chain was still thickly waxed. Your lad saw that, didn't he? Now then, what else … Oh, yes; spots of corrosion on both taps. Splashes, probably. Slight discolouration of vitreous enamel consistent with submersion in fairly highly concentrated sulphuric acid. Acid traces on bathroom floor …'

Warlock's finger moved slowly down the page. 'Wax on bath corresponded with solid deposit in basin in dining-room sideboard …' He looked up. 'Queer slip, that: leaving the thing about. Never mind, that's not my pigeon.' He read on. 'No distinguishable fingerprints on basin, damn it – still, it would have been asking a bit much.'

'Drains,' announced Warlock after a brief pause. 'We didn't do too badly with drains.' While still keeping his eyes on the report, he felt for the black box and slipped its catch. 'Analysis of contents of drain trap established presence of unusual quantities of fat and carbon compounds, possibly of animal derivation, also distinct calcium traces … you're with me there, I suppose, squire?'

Purbright nodded. 'The late Mr Hopjoy, I presume.' He received an approving beam from the expert.

'Mind you, you mustn't get the idea that anything like actual identification is possible from this sort of thing. It's all a bit tentative.'

'Oh, quite.'

'But circumstantially impressive, all the same.' Warlock sounded eager to please. 'Naturally, there'd been some dilution of what went into the drain trap. Fat and acid tests were absolutely conclusive, though. I'm only sorry there wasn't anything exciting in the solid line – plastic buttons, gold teeth fillings – you know.'

'Pity.'

Warlock lifted back the lid of his box. He drew a test tube from a small rack at the back of it. 'This has flummoxed us, I admit. It had caught in that little grill thing under the plug.'

Purbright turned the tube round in his hand. Within it he saw a knotted loop of whitish, translucent fibre. He held it to the light. 'Animal, vegetable or mineral?'

'Oh, mineral,' said Warlock. 'Almost certainly nylon.'

'Out of a nailbrush, perhaps?'

'Too long. Anyway, it wouldn't be joined up like that. It's not out of a brush of any kind. Nobody at the lab had a clue.'

'Are you worried about it?'

Warlock scowled indignantly and whisked the tube out of Purbright's grasp. 'Of course I'm worried about it. We haven't been foxed by anything in this line since the Retford fly-paper case. Do you know, we spent two months making inquiries at jewellers about that cuff-link in old Mrs Hargreaves's duodenum. In the end we traced it to the bloody surgeon who did the autopsy.'

He put the test tube back in its rack. 'Oh, we'll get some joy out of this, don't you worry. I'm sending it off to the top bods in the artificial fibre industry. I expect they'll check it with their gauge records or something.'

'It may be quite unconnected with the case, of course,' ventured Purbright, who was beginning to find Warlock's forensic rhapsody a trifle wearing.

'Five pounds to a gnat's navel it had absolutely nothing to do with it, squire. Elimination, though ... that's what counts with us, elimination.' He looked again at his report. 'Now then; where were we? Ah, bloodstains ...'

There were six sites of staining. The bathroom floor had been spotted. The wall splashes had proved, as expected, positive. Blood accounted for the mark on the razor blade found in the bathroom cabinet. Then there was the hammer head. Finally, careful search had disclosed a few smears on the stair carpet and on the concrete floor of the garage.

The last two had lent themselves admirably to the process of elimination. They were not of human origin. All the others were and they belonged to the same common 'O' group.

'I don't quite see how the razor blade fits in,' said Purbright. 'It's hardly likely to have been used as a weapon. I mean you don't fell a bloke with a hammer and then cut his throat: that would be sheer ostentation. Anyway, we should have found more mess, surely?'

Warlock watched him with the secretly gleeful air of a conjuror whose audience falls for diversion while the best part of his trick is in preparation.

'I told you, didn't I, that this case is absolutely marvellous?' His eyes gleamed. 'Now then; what do you think of this?'

Purbright picked up the large photograph that had been slid triumphantly before him.

It appeared to be of a huge, round butcher's block on to which a handful of canes had been carelessly tossed. The canes were partly embedded in a thick, tarry substance, spread irregularly over the surface of the block. They stuck out, some straight, some curving, at varying angles.

'This one's been pulled up even farther.' Warlock tossed down a second photograph. The canes had become long, segmented stovepipes, jutting from some sort of dune, coarsely granular in texture. Purbright was reminded of surrealist seashore paintings.

'The hammer head,' announced Warlock.

'Ah, yes.'

Warlock waited. 'Of course, you see what's wrong.'

The inspector held the second enlargement at arm's length and squinted judiciously. 'To be perfectly honest …'

Impatiently, scornfully almost, Warlock leaned over and jabbed his finger at the stovepipes. 'No crushing. No skin. No follicles.'

The triple negation sounded like a maximum sentence without possibility of appeal. Purbright nodded meekly. 'You're perfectly right, of course. Not a follicle in sight.'

Warlock sighed and took up a relatively relaxed pose behind Purbright's chair. He pointed, more gently this time, at the prints.

'You see, squire, it's reasonable to expect that hairs are going to stick to a hammer when it's used to bash somebody's head in. But they get squeezed between two hard surfaces – steel and bone – for a fraction of a second before the skull gives way. So naturally they ought to show damage. These don't.

'Another thing: the hairs, or some of them, are bound to come out, roots and all. Plus the odd bit of skin, of course. But in this case … well, you can see for yourself.'

Purbright studied the photographs a little longer and said: 'Obviously, we'll have to come back to these. But perhaps you'd like to run over what's left of the other things first.'

The remainder of the report was straightforward enough. The broken glass unearthed from the garden included large fragments easily identifiable as portions of a commercial acid carboy, whose protective basket of iron strapping had been found in a wardrobe (Purbright loyally forbore from mentioning Love's encounter with that article). Glass splinters on the second hammer, that left in the garage, clearly indicated its having been used to smash the carboy.

Two sets of fingerprints were recurrent throughout the house. One set corresponded with prints at Periam's shop. The other, presumably, was Hopjoy's. There had been found no print belonging to either man which could be considered of special significance in relation to whatever had happened in the bathroom. The surfaces of the hammer shafts, the razor blade, and the pieces of carboy had yielded nothing.

Microscopic examination of hairs taken from combs in Periam's bedroom and shop and from clothing in a cupboard in his lodger's room had virtually settled the origin of those on the hammer. They were almost certainly Hopjoy's.

'There you are, squire. Make what you like of that lot.'

Purbright rubbed his chin reflectively. 'You've certainly been thorough.'

Warlock beamed. He tossed up an imaginary tennis ball and thwacked it through the window.

'It's just as well,' said Purbright, 'that I didn't clap Periam in irons this morning. I suppose I couldn't have been blamed if I had. Yet there was something rather pat about the set-up at that house. It was too much to expect a nice conclusive lab report ...' he tapped the photographs – '... with follicles.'

'Sorry.'

'Those hairs, then, were ...'

Warlock winked, turned two fingers into a pair of scissors and snipped off an invisible forelock.

*

Purbright carried Warlock's report to the Chief Constable not in confidence that Mr Chubb possessed a superiority of intellect consonant with his rank but rather as a man with a problem will seek out some simple natural scene, the contemplation of which seems to set free part of his mind to delve more effectually towards a solution.

Thus, while he gazed at the gentle, dignified vacuity of Mr Chubb's face, the inspector mentally weighed and dissected each fact as he passed it on.

Mr Chubb, as usual, was leaning elegantly against his fireplace. He seemed never to sit down except at home, and then almost exclusively at meal times. 'Harcourt,' his wife once averred, 'even watches television standing up; I think his mother must have been frightened by Edward the Seventh.'

The Chief Constable gave a delicate, dry cough. 'Do I understand, Mr Purbright, that you feel an arrest would be unwise at this stage?'

'Ah, I thought that might be your reaction, sir. It's this queer business of the hammer that's spoiling everything.'

'It strikes me,' said Mr Chubb, 'as a singularly unnecessary complication. Do we really have to take Warlock's word that the thing was deliberately contrived?'

'I'm afraid we do. And the case won't hang together until we can explain why the murderer went to that particular piece of trouble. He'd prepared to dispose of the corpse; the logical thing was to erase all other signs of the crime – wash away bloodstains, burn the ligature or bury the knife or get rid of the gun, wipe off fingerprints, and so on. But no, he actually manufactured some evidence of violence by cutting off a few of the victim's hairs and sticking them on a hammer head with a dab of his blood. You notice the choice of hiding place, incidentally – under the bath – accessible to methodical searchers, yet just not obvious enough to arouse suspicion of a deliberate plant.'

'I hate to see subtlety showing through these affairs, Mr Purbright. Murder is such a beastly business in the first place. It becomes positively crawly when you have to strain a decent intelligence to sort it out. And nowadays, I'm afraid, the better the address the more distasteful the crime turns out to be. Odd, that, isn't it?'

'You're thinking of Beatrice Avenue, of course …'

'Well, it is quite a nice road. I remember old Abbott and his sister used to live in that place with a yellow gate, up at the park end.' He paused, frowning. 'You know, this is going to drop the values a bit.'

Purbright observed a short, respectful silence. He resumed: 'One thing is abundantly clear: the murder wasn't done on the spur of the moment. If Periam had killed Hopjoy during that quarrel and without premeditation, how could he have set about getting rid of the body so efficiently? A carboy of acid isn't something you keep handy around the house, and you'd hardly be able to nip out and buy one at that time of night.'

'One might steal it,' suggested the Chief Constable. 'It would be a good time for that.'

Purbright acknowledged the possibility, but thought that burglary on top of murder was cramming rather a lot into one night. 'The acid must have been obtained be-forehand and hidden in readiness – not necessarily at the house, although there's an inspection pit in the garage that would have served very well.'

Mr Chubb nodded sagely. 'I grant premeditation.'

'Which leads us,' Purbright said, 'to two further points of some importance. Firstly, the chances of Hopjoy's hav-ing been killed and, shall we say, liquidated by anyone not actually living in the same house must be considered very remote indeed. The whole situation, before and after the crime, demanded what might be termed residential qual-ifications – privacy, time, freedom from the curiosity of neighbours, knowledge of the house itself. Periam really is the only candidate, you know, sir.'

The Chief Constable thoughtfully inspected the lapel of his jacket. 'Put like that … I suppose there wouldn't be much point in propounding the roving maniac, much as one would like to. I can't say I know this Periam my-self, but he's a decent type by all accounts. Why on earth should he want to do such a frightful thing?'

'Precisely, sir. That's the second point I wanted to bring out. His motive must have been of pathological intensity.'

'Any money involved?'

'Far from it. Hopjoy seems to have left nothing but debts. Even the car was going to be snatched back by the hire purchase people.'

'Debts?' Mr Chubb stared. 'But what about the work he was supposed to be doing? I mean, a man in his position would never risk …'

'Oh, but he did, sir. You haven't forgotten the Arliss business, surely.'

'Arliss?'

'The tailor. He wanted us to do Hopjoy for false pretences. We'd quite a job cooling him down.'

Mr Chubb made show of searching his memory. 'Ah ... that was Hopjoy, was it?'

'It was. He told Arliss that the suit had been impounded by MI5 because one of his machinists was suspected of passing micro-film in hollow fly buttons.'

'And did they get the fellow?'

'Hopjoy, you mean, sir?'

'No, the fellow who was doing that button trick. Nobody thought to tell me afterwards what happened.'

It dawned on Purbright that the point of the affair had eluded Mr Chubb completely. 'I suppose,' he said, 'that he was investigated. Probably put on less sensitive work – cuffs, maybe.'

When the Chief Constable spoke again, it was with the careful tone of a man aware of his own inadequate sense of the ridiculous and determined not to betray it by rebuking flippancy. Mr Chubb did not so much mind his subordinates being impertinent – that was, after all, a form of acknowledging inferiority; what he dreaded was that any of them might say something really funny without his recognising it.

'Be that as it may,' said Mr Chubb. 'I agree that robbery seems out. Do you suppose Periam was being threatened, then? Paying the other chap money, I mean?'

'That's unlikely, sir. We've checked Periam's accounts; there's no indication of extortion.'

Mr Chubb gazed upwards. There came to him a thought he found difficult to express. 'One doesn't like to be uncharitable,' he began, 'but perhaps we shouldn't ignore ... Well, two fellows on their own in the same house ...'

Purbright rescued him. 'The record leaves no doubt of Hopjoy's having been almost aggressively heterosexual, sir.'

'Oh, was he? I'm glad to hear it. One knows that sort of thing goes on, of course … Still, I wouldn't like to think of you having to fish in those waters.'

The inspector was glancing through his notebook record of the conversations at Brockleston. 'Do you know the Neptune Hotel, sir?' he asked, without looking up.

'I think I went into the place once,' said Mr Chubb, guardedly. 'A bit on the flashy side.'

'Decidedly,' Purbright agreed. 'It struck me as a slightly off-key choice for a honeymoon. Periam was mother-ridden, though; perhaps the Neptune appealed as a symbol of emancipation. Also it could have been in line with his role as seducer; that was Hopjoy's girl he married, you know.'

'Really?'

'Which is another curious feature. One would have thought that it was Hopjoy who had cause to kill Periam, not the other way round. Husbands are sometimes eliminated from triangles, but I don't think I can recall a case of fiancécide. Anyway, it's the rejected suitor who is apt to be violent, not his successor.'

'Do you think the girl knows what's been going on?'

Purbright considered. 'I'm not at all sure. There's a certain ruthlessness about her. I wonder if you can imagine a bed-hopping Sunday school teacher …'

It was evident from Mr Chubb's expression that he couldn't.

'What I mean is that she looks almost frumpish – unfashionable clothes, no make-up, dreadful hair style – yet underneath she seems to be continually flexing and

shuffling. She gives a most disconcerting impression of …
well, appetite.'

'She doesn't sound a very nice young woman. She *is* young, I presume?'

'Younger than her husband, certainly. I find it hard to understand why she dropped Hopjoy – very much the accomplished buck, by all accounts – in favour of a man like Periam.'

'Women,' stated Mr Chubb, 'are unpredictable.'

Purbright recognised that the Chief Constable had received as much confusing information as he could stomach at one session. He picked up the report and photographs. 'Is there anything more at the moment, sir?'

'I don't think so. We shall just have to carry on ploughing our furrow, you know. See what turns up.'

'Very well, sir.' Purbright walked to the door.

'Oh, by the way, Mr Purbright …' Mr Chubb disengaged himself from the mantelpiece and meticulously slipped his finger-ends into his jacket pockets. 'I had a chat with Major Ross this morning. I suppose he and Mr Pumphrey are trained to take a rather less mundane view of these affairs. Of course, they do operate in a wider sphere than ours. I have the impression that they readily conceive of possibilities which you and I might dismiss as excessively dramatic …'

'Yes, sir?'

Mr Chubb traced a pattern on the carpet with one well-shined toecap. 'Yes, well I think I ought to tell you that Major Ross and his colleague don't share your opinion that Periam is the man responsible. In their parlance, he is described as "cleared", and they are looking much farther afield.'

'I don't think we should take exception to that, sir. I'm glad of any assistance they can give.'

'Oh, quite so. I'm sure you don't regard their co-operation ungenerously. No, that isn't what I'm anxious about. It's simply that outsiders tend to underestimate our people, Mr Purbright – in the country districts particularly. We don't want these gentlemen running into any unpleasantness, do we? After all, they are our guests, in a sense.'

Purbright nodded. 'I'll do my best to look after them.'

Mr Chubb achieved a smile. 'I thought I'd better mention it. Major Ross did say something about making a few inquiries in Mumblesby, as a matter of fact.'

'Merry Mumblesby,' said Purbright, reflectively. He opened the door.

Chapter Eleven

'INGENIOUS,' ROSS SAID. He lifted the narrow rectangle of paper aloft with his pipe stem, held it in draped balance a moment, then withdrew the pipe sharply. The paper side-slipped twice and floated to rest on the table by Pumphrey's elbow.

'Chubb was perfectly correct, you see. It *is* a betting slip.' Ross lengthened his face in mimicry. '"We collect plenty of those, Mr Ross: they are merely symptoms of one of our little local weaknesses." Poor old Chubb. Tretnikov or Dzarbol would have three of him for breakfast. It isn't innocent things like bus tickets or jam labels that pass unchallenged, but the obviously illegal ones. Betting slips? Of course they are taken for betting slips. What else could they be?'

Pumphrey peered at the paper earnestly, pulling his right ear lobe as if it put him in circuit with an electronic scanner. 'Five shillings each way Needlework Hurst Park 4.30 Peter Piper,' he read in an unpunctuated monotone.

'Pre-selected pseudonymic code: impossible to break. We needn't waste time on it.' Ross held out his hand.

'Hold on a minute ...' Pumphrey's ear became tauter, redder. He muttered the message again to himself, then tapped the paper. 'Needlework,' he said with emphasis and looked up.

'Name of the horse. I've checked. It's running in the 4.30 all right.' Ross spoke mechanically. His attention was held by the bright, blood-flooded lobe of Pumphrey's ear. He pictured the fearful rending tongs fashioned by the Cracow goldsmith whom fate, and an ungrateful party secretariat, had made their first victim; 'unfeatured' was the word that had been sardonically entered in his prison hospital record.

'Yes, but needlework ... examine it association-wise. Needle ... sewing ... thimble ... Thimble Bay.'

Interest glimmered in Ross's eye, but only briefly. He shook his head. 'Attractive, Harry, but just that fraction too obvious. No, what matters is that our friends' main communication channels are being confirmed. It's our immediate job to follow them. I'll say this for F.7: he left some pretty positive leads.'

Pumphrey watched Ross place the betting slip in his briefcase. 'I've sent a screening requisition on Anderson, of course.'

'Anderson? Oh, old dot and carry one. Good. Chubb's fellows have him tabbed simply as a bookie's runner, but I expected that. They probably think nuclear disarmament's another name for the Oxford Movement.' Ross looked at the ivory and zirconium face of his wristwatch. 'Just nice time,' he observed, 'to pay Mrs Bernadette Croll a call before Farmer Croll homeward plods from his turnip patch or whatever. Coming along for the drive?'

*

Mumblesby was a hamlet of fourteen houses, a decrepit church and a ruined water mill. Its founders seemed to have tucked it quite deliberately into a green fold of the hills so that no one else should find it. Even today, when a main road to the coast ran within a quarter of a mile of its crumbling gables and rat-ridden thatch, Mumblesby still crouched in its valley unseen and unsought.

Speeding silently away from Mumblesby was a huge Bentley with a prow of gunmetal, whose pilot, Ross, remarked to his companion: 'About another four minutes should do it.' But the car, painstakingly misdirected by humorous rustics, continued to sail through the high, greenish-white foam of cow parsley and past banks empurpled with campion before a signpost confirmed Pumphrey's suspicion that they were about to re-enter the outskirts of Flaxborough.

Ross grasped the situation immediately. He neither slacked pace nor changed direction. 'We'll stop at the first decent-sized stationers and get an ordnance survey map,' he announced. 'You shouldn't have taken those fellows literally, you know, Harry. I thought they were having you on.'

Pumphrey's lean and diligent face swung round indignantly. It had been Ross who had taken charge of what he called the 'peasant-parley'. 'But look, I didn't ...' Ross quickly smiled and patted his arm. 'My dear Harry, you're far too easily drawn into categorical protestations; it doesn't do, you know.'

At the newsagents where the required map was produced, Ross bought himself a fudge and roasted hazelnut bar. Pumphrey he treated to a sixpenny Yummie – honey-spun raisins in a cushion of chocolate praline, twice whipped for lightness.

Twenty minutes later, the Bentley rocked to a halt among roadside flowers, just clear of the narrow lane that pierced Mumblesby's encircling groves of ash and elm. Ross examined the map. 'I'll go up to the farm; it's about two hundred yards up there on the right, according to this. You stay here if you like, unless you want to nose around what there is of a village.'

Ross turned from the tree-vaulted lane, where the air was cool and green as old glass, on to a flint work road that ran straight between brown, sun-hardened fields. The earth was yielding the first clenched leaves of a potato crop, but still so few that no pattern of its sowing could be discerned. At the end of the track, the grey brick and funereal slate of a Victorian farmhouse defied the sun to soften their sour angularity. The older out-buildings, preserved when the original house was demolished and replaced, were roofed with red pantiles. They looked like robust, bibulous suitors attending upon a sick widow.

A few chickens pecked in the dust of the untidy yard, the only other occupant of which was a mired and malevolent-looking goose. Ross stepped carefully over the wheel ruts that still held in their depths the foetid residue of winter rains and seepage from the crew-yard, opened a wicket in the wire fence enclosing the house and its narrow strip of garden, and walked up to the front door.

His knock produced a hollow, unpromising reverberation, as if the house had sullenly murmured 'go away' in its sleep. He waited, knocked again, and listened. From somewhere fairly distant came the sound of music. The door remained shut. Ross reached for the big brown enamelled knob. It twisted loosely and without effect.

'Are you the killer?'

Ross spun round. The soft, rather bored voice had delivered its appalling question as flatly as if it had asked him

120

for a match. 'People usually come round to the back, you know. You could have waited here all day.'

'Am I the *what*?'

The girl, unaware of the singularity of her accomplishment in having startled, of all people, Ross, looked him up and down. 'No, you're not Mr Rassmussen, are you? I think he's a Dane or something. Anyway, he's the killer from Gelding Marsh. Ours has a septic thumb.'

'I see.' Ross tried to imagine a rational connection between thumbs and assassination. 'You mean he's a strangler?'

'Don't be silly. You don't strangle pigs.' There was no amusement in her voice.

'Naturally not. Nevertheless, I'm not your Mr Rassmussen. You *are* Mrs Croll, though, I take it.'

'That's right. Why?'

'Do you think we might go inside? I'd like to talk to you.'

The girl subjected him again to doubtful, sulky scrutiny. This time, Ross returned her stare, appraising the lumpish yet indefinably provocative face, a throat fair-fleshed and smooth within the opening of a wine-red linen shirt that outlined narrow shoulders and gently understated the existence of breasts.

It was Mrs Croll's gaze that turned aside first, but the gesture carried no suggestion of defeat or embarrassment. Nor, as she walked before him round the side of the house, did she seem to divine or care that his sensual preoccupation had been deepened by the anterior viewpoint and by the addition of movement. She was perfectly familiar with the standard of her charms – she could have defined it instantly as '34–23–38' – and her faith in their effect was as simple and absolute as if all these parts bore the tattooed warranty 'as seen on TV'.

Television, Ross discovered when they entered the small, over-furnished parlour, was the source of the music he had heard. As she walked through the doorway, the girl's eyes sought automatically the steel-blue radiance of the screen in the corner. They slotted at once into focus as though held upon invisible antennae springing in parallel from the set, and abdicated responsibility for all else. Thus, as she felt her way to a couch in the room's centre, her body moved round pieces of furniture with the cautious, sensitive independence of the blind.

Ross watched the foot that felt for and pushed aside a stool in her path. Its toes, half revealed by the green suede shoe's shallow cut, squeezed like plump baby mice against their nylon caul. Her instep, he noticed, was gracefully arched but too puffy to display the delicate bone structure that he would claim to have been taught to value by the bagnio-masters of southeastern Turkey. The ankle was similarly spoiled, yet the failing was its very merit, for it hastened with impatience the upward progress of Ross's scrutiny to a limb he deemed so eloquent of erotic responsiveness that his fingers involuntarily curved in sympathy. Especially compelling was the flexed roundness of muscle, behind and a little above the knee – the thigh's beginning – that gleamed momentarily as the couch arm caught at the girl's skirt.

She arranged herself among the cushions like a florid signature. Ross, for whom she spared no further glance, sat uninvited in a chair a few inches away, his back to the television set.

The girl spoke first, but without turning her head. 'Well, what was it you wanted?'

'To talk to you.'

'My husband handles all the farm business. Anyway, you're wasting your time if you're selling something; he's satisfied with everything he gets now.'

'That I can believe.' Ross watched her face. She was smiling faintly.

'Is your husband about?'

'Naturally. You didn't think he worked in an office. He's down on the bottom field. Harrowing.'

'It must be.'

The girl suppressed a giggle, then frowned. 'I don't like sarcastic people. If you'll just tell me what you want ...'

'I'm trying to trace a friend of mine.'

'Someone round here, you mean?'

'I think he's been here.'

'What's his name?' She leaned along the back of the couch and stretched to turn down the volume of the set. She could just reach the knob with the tips of her fingers. Ross noted appreciatively the hardening of the nearer buttock into the semblance of a lute. 'Hopjoy,' he said, 'Brian Hopjoy.'

'Never heard of him.' She settled again into the cushions, drawing one leg closely beneath her and allowing the other to trail to the floor. Ross abandoned himself to a familiar sense of wonder at the contrast between a stocking's steely, slippery containment and the petal-white vulnerability of overtopping flesh. He once had thought the Can-Can a vulgar and pseudo-, indeed anti-sensual concession to callow tourists. Now he understood its truth. It was a sermon upon the insubstantiality of what separated the pretentiousness and artificial properties of civilisation from venal reality – a division no greater than a garter's width.

Ross leaned forward in his chair. 'Mrs Croll ...'

Abstractedly she felt for her skirt hem and tugged it down to her knee. Her fingers straightened and travelled on, in the lightest self-caress; then she raised the hand and held it towards him. He grasped her wrist and experienced a sort of contentment in exploring, with one finger-tip, its complex of fragile bones.

'You might not have known him as Hopjoy,' Ross said.

'Mightn't I?' Still she stared at the screen; only the tiniest twitch of the hand Ross held contradicted her attitude of absolute indifference to what existed outside it. He slackened his hand and extended it slowly, her forearm slipping through the cupped fingers until his thumb nestled in the soft, warm hollow of the arm's crook. A pulse – his own or hers, he did not know – stirred gently within the area of contact; it seemed a microcosmic prelude to …

'Here, we're wasting time.' He withdrew his hand and reached into an inner pocket.

She looked round, startled by his brusqueness. Immediately she saw the photograph, her eyes widened. 'Is that your friend?'

'Tell me about him.'

She pouted. 'Why should I? I don't know who you are. You haven't even got his name right, anyway.'

Ross saw the look she gave the photograph of Hopjoy; it was compounded of fondness and a curious detachment, like that of a marksman turning over a shot bird with his foot.

'Names,' he said, 'don't matter much in our game, Mrs Croll. I don't care what you called the man, nor what he meant to you …'

'And just what are you insinuating?' She had put on a tradesmen's entrance voice. Ross decided that he recognised the dissimulation of the bored middle-class wife, hungering for sexual humiliation. 'Your antics in your husband's hay-loft are rather beside the point, my dear. I am interested solely in what brought Mr Hopjoy to this farm and in what he learned here. Now perhaps we understand each other.'

She had risen at his first words and stood now in what he diagnosed as trembling enjoyment of the insult he had offered. The rigidity of her indignation, he noticed, thrust into satisfying prominence a narrow, muscular belly and slightly flattened breasts like burglar alarms.

Mrs Croll turned, switched off the television set as if for ever, and faced him again. 'There is nothing,' she announced coldly, 'in the relationship of Mr Trevelyan and I that is any of your damn business.' She paused. 'So damn you!'

Ross felt a twinge of pity. The clumsiness and inadequate sonority of the retort, its little grammatical discord, betrayed the girl's uncertainty. He smiled at her. Into the suddenly silent room threaded the thin, clattering whine of a distant tractor.

'Trevelyan, you say?'

'Howard Trevelyan.' She pronounced the words defiantly and with schoolgirl relish.

'Sit down.' He took out his pipe and ruminantly fingered the rim of its bowl. The girl hesitated, then moved farther off and sat on a straight-backed chair in an attitude of prim exasperation.

Not looking at her, Ross said: 'You are going to have to trust me, Bernadette. I could tell you my name – it's Ross, as a matter of fact – and the nature of my work, but there really would be no point in doing so. I can neither prove my identity nor give you convincing evidence of my profession. If I could, it would cease to be my profession. You don't understand. Naturally. You are not expected to understand. But at least let me assure you that what might seem to you duplicity and mystification are terribly necessary.'

He glanced at her face, which had become more bewildered than angry. 'Don't worry, you'll not get hurt. I can see no need for your husband to learn anything you don't wish him to learn concerning, er, Trevelyan' – he lingered sternly over the name as if he personally disapproved of it – 'provided you are frank with me.'

'Are you a detective, or something?'

He considered, smiling again. 'A something – I think we'd better settle for that.'

'Are you working with Howard?'

'We have certain objectives in common.'

Mrs Croll looked at the door. Then she crossed the room and settled in her habitual place on the sofa. Her face was turned fully towards Ross. She ran her tongue-tip over her lips before she spoke.

'Has anything happened to him?'

Ross shrugged. 'We can't trace him just at the moment.'

'He's not back in hospital?'

Ross went quickly back over his mental copy of the Hopjoy reports. There had been a spell in hospital. Attacked with iron bar. Assailant thought to be Bulgarian. Never traced; probably smuggled out of Flaxborough dock. For victim, special compensation grant. But all that was some time ago. 'No,' said Ross, 'I think he got over that all right.'

'I was terribly worried. That's where he came down ...' She nodded towards the window. 'Right on top of an old kennel that used to stand there. I thought Ben had killed him ...'

'Ben?'

'My husband. He threw Howard out of the bedroom window.'

Ross stared at her, trying to bore through to the motives for the lie. Was she simply the willing victim of sexual fantasy? Or had someone coached her in a deliberately descreditable explanation of Hopjoy's injuries?

'Tell me about it.'

She raised a hand and moved the middle finger lightly round the braided coil of her hair. The bunched strands shone, thought Ross, like the newly baked croissants of the Orgérus Region. Her frown was doubtful. 'I don't think I ought to say any more. I promised Howard ...'

He leaned forward and grasped her shoulder. Tightening the grip, he saw a flicker of gratification in her eyes before the heavy lids drew down in white, lazy assent. The long kiss he gave her was an interrogation subtly wavering on the borders of brutality. Before it was over, she half opened her eyes and moaned through his teeth, like a prisoner entreating merciful execution.

Ross disengaged with controlled, skilful gradualness. As might a superb driver cast his eye over his engine after a trial burst of speed, he made a brief inward check of the muscular and glandular apparatus of his prowess. He dismissed as imaginary a touch of breathlessness, a fleeting impression of cramp in his right shoulder. No, these were nothing; the old mastery was unimpaired. He prepared to inaugurate the second, the behold-my-need phase. As he gazed earnestly down into her eyes, he set off at irregular but artistic intervals a tiny tic at the corner of his now tightly compressed mouth. He raised one eyebrow in mute request for licence, while simultaneously contracting the other to indicate the irresistibility of his desire. This refined and difficult performance had never failed to win compliance with the subsequent phase of his technique, the tactile assessment and breach of dress fastenings and his hands' assured colonisation of their discoveries.

But at this point Ross's calculated progression was disrupted utterly and with no hope of the re-establishment of his control. With a cry like that of a teased and hungry seal seizing a dangled fish, Bernadette suddenly arched and twisted her body, pincered him between iron-like legs, and bore him to the floor, where she proceeded to chew his neck, shoulder, and ear with every indication of determination and delight. Within seconds, the rhythm of seduction had been checked, perverted and monstrously accelerated in reverse. Through the hot clamour of Bernadette's lovemaking, Ross seemed to hear, as if from outer space, the thin, mocking laughter of enemies.

*

An hour and ten minutes later, Ross was making his way back to the car while Bernadette Croll, her face as animated as a calf's, watched a pan of potatoes and cabbage frying for her husband's tea.

Ross felt like the survivor of an ambush. He glanced wearily at the peewits that glided and side-slipped above his head and plunged to the furrows in an untidy, tumbling descent as if they, like him, had been drained of impetus. Yet he felt neither self-pity nor rancour. What mattered now was to sift from the more embarrassing memories of the past hour the story about Hopjoy that he had been able to extract from his conquest during the few and brief periods of respite from her importunities.

Hopjoy, as his own reports indicated, had called at the Crolls' farm in the first instance to make inquiries about some European labourers who were employed there. On that and subsequent visits, it was Mrs Croll whom he had seen. The farmer, Benjamin Croll, spent all daylight hours in his fields except at mealtimes, which were strictly predictable. Mrs Croll had told 'Howard Trevelyan' what she knew and what since she had been able, on his instructions, to find out about the three workers, but this amounted to little and seemed innocent. It had been nice, though, to see Howard once or twice in each otherwise killingly boring week and she had been thrilled and proud when he told her – on his third visit – that he was a British counter-espionage agent.

Ross dwelt a moment on this somewhat surprising circumstance. He did not think the girl was lying when she said the confidence had come from Hopjoy. There must, therefore, have been some very compelling reason for the breaking of so elementary a rule of security. Had Hopjoy hoped thereby to draw his quarry into the open? To offer himself as bait? If so, it meant the situation had become critical.

Such a likelihood was strengthened by Hopjoy's urgent assertion to the girl, whom obviously he had decided to accept as an active ally, that his life was in danger. She had responded by hiding him in her bedroom on a number of occasions when the absence of her husband at Flaxborough market might have encouraged the enemy to arrange a convenient accident.

The accident when it did come was of entirely unexpected authorship. Not sharing his wife's knowledge of the situation at the farm, Croll had returned early from a cancelled ram sale and gone straight up to the bedroom to change his clothes. He had brushed introductions aside, and, according to Mrs Croll, 'behaved dreadfully'.

Ross opened the gate into the lane and thoughtfully latched it behind him. Who, in fact, had been Hopjoy's assailant? Was it really Croll, the misunderstanding husband, who, if his wife's story were to be credited, had regretted his impulsiveness, picked the unconscious man from the roof of the dog kennel and driven him to hospital with a tale of a fall from a stack?

Or had Bernadette's account – so sharply at variance with the F.7 reports – been concocted and rehearsed in fear of reprisals from the organisation that had spirited back to the East the practitioner with the iron bar?

Within fifty yards of the Bentley, in which he saw glimmering the pallid paraboloid of Pumphrey's skull, Ross paused to listen. The sound of the tractor engine, to which he had kept tuned a wary ear during the whole time he had spent in the farmhouse, was in the air no longer. Its sudden extinction loosed a third and startling possibility into his brain.

Was it Benjamin Croll himself who had been the real object of Hopjoy's investigations? Whose agent had struck too clumsily? Who then prepared in person and with deadly thoroughness to finalise Hopjoy's elimination at the villa in Beatrice Avenue?

Chapter Twelve

MR ALFRED BLOSSOM, proprietor of the South Circuit Garage, Flaxborough, received with considerable scepticism his foreman's report that one of four carboys of battery acid had disappeared from the yard at the side of the servicing bay. 'Even our blokes couldn't lose a thing like that,' he declared. 'And who the hell would want to pinch it? You'd better count them again.'

But not all Mr Blossom's homely humour, developed over long years of stonewalling the complaints of milched motorists, could alter the fact that where four carboys had stood there were now only three. So he stared awhile at the empty space, bent to retrieve a small object that shone in the shadow of the next caged and straw-pillowed bottle, and put through a telephone call to the police.

There the matter rested until Inspector Purbright's request for a check on all local garages, wholesale chemists, and factories for news of missing sulphuric acid struck a chord in the memory of the clerk who had filed the peculiar little item from South Circuit.

Purbright found Mr Blossom an affable informant, graced with that air of sincerity and solicitude characteristic of the habitual inflator of invoices.

'It was the queerest thing,' said Mr Blossom. 'I mean, we've had stuff disappear before. It goes on all the time, as a matter of fact. Between ourselves, I don't make much of it. Put it down as wastage – sort of evaporation, you know. But a bloody great thing like that … Dangerous too. And it's not as if you could flog it.' A good foot shorter than the policeman, he stood with his head tilted sharply upward like a bespectacled mole.

'Have you any idea of how it could have been taken?'

'Oh, in a car or on a truck, I suppose. People are always in and out of a place like this. We don't watch everybody all the time. Some poor barmy sod probably took a fancy to the thing and heaved it into his boot when no one was looking.' He spread his hands and smiled forgiveness.

'They're pretty heavy, though, aren't they?'

'About a hundredweight apiece. A fairly strong bloke could manage one on his own.'

'When you talk of people being in and out, you mean customers, I suppose.'

'That's right. They just bring their cars into, the yard there or back them into the shop. Some of them might want to help themselves to the air line, or a grease gun. We don't bother so long as they're not in the way.'

'Free and easy.'

Mr Blossom shrugged. 'Why not? You can't run a garage like a jewellers.'

'You feel that this thing must have been pinched during the daytime?'

'I really haven't thought about it. As I said, I expect some idiot whipped it on the spur of the moment. He wouldn't do that at night, would he? In the dark, I mean.'

Purbright walked to the corner of the L-shaped yard, looked round it, and returned. Mr Blossom forestalled comment. 'Oh, yes, it's open to the street. There's nothing to stop anybody coming this far at any time, if they wanted to.'

'Or if they knew these carboys were kept here and happened to want one.'

Mr Blossom slightly relaxed his smile to signify regret of the world's waywardness and blinked. Purbright saw the set of pale blue concentric circles dissolve from the thick, upturned lenses and then spread back, more watery than before.

'Do you happen to keep a list of your customers, Mr Blossom?'

'We do, yes.'

'I wonder if I might take a quick look at it.'

Mr Blossom turned and led the way across the shop and up an open wooden staircase to his office. He pulled out the drawer of a small box file and graciously stepped aside.

The names were in alphabetical order. Purbright saw that Hopjoy's card had a little scarlet disc gummed neatly to the upper left-hand corner. There were a few others similarly decorated. The name Periam was not listed.

'May I ask what the red circles mean?'

Mr Blossom peered innocently at the open file. 'Oh, it's just a sort of private mark we use in the accounting system ...'

'Bad payers?'

'Well ...' Mr Blossom spread his hands. 'Oh, by the way ...' He unlocked and opened the top drawer of his desk and handed Purbright a heavy cigarette lighter. 'Found it on the scene of the crime. None of my chaps had lost it.'

Purbright turned the lighter over in his hand. It looked expensively durable and efficient but bore neither decoration nor brand name. 'Might be helpful. Thanks.' He slipped the lighter into his pocket and pencilled a note of receipt.

'By the way, I notice you've done work on a car belonging to a man called Hopjoy, of Beatrice Avenue. Does he always bring it in himself?'

'The Armstrong, you mean. No, not always. A friend of his drives as well, The servicing's not done in his name, though.'

'What's the friend called?'

Mr Blossom wrinkled his helpful nose. 'Perry, I think ... no, Periam. He keeps a cigarette shop.'

But doesn't smoke, Purbright added to himself. 'All right, Mr Blossom. We'll let you know if your magnum turns up.'

Not to be outdone in jocularity, Mr Blossom sang out in rasping baritone: 'And if one green bottle should accidentally fall ...' and wrung Purbright's hand like an old friend.

*

Back at police headquarters, the inspector found Ross and Pumphrey awaiting him. The Chief Constable, faced with a bewildering variety of requests for information about a one-legged snooker player, a barber, a farmer, and a Scandinavian pig slaughterer, had gravely assured his questioners that 'Mr Purbright handles all that sort of thing' and gone home to do some gardening.

Purbright listened attentively until his visitors, judging him to have been put squarely in the picture, invited him to deliver reciprocal revelation.

He rose. 'I think, gentlemen, that the best thing will be to call in a couple of our local experts.'

Pumphrey looked startled. 'I don't know about that, inspector. You realise all this is top secret ...' He glanced at Ross.

Purbright leaned against the door frame. He sighed. 'I don't pretend to be an encyclopaedia, you know. Some of my men have a much wider range; they might save you a lot of time.'

'That's all right, Purbright,' Ross said. 'I'm sure you can question your chaps in a way that won't set any rabbits away.'

When the inspector re-entered the room five minutes later, he was accompanied by Sergeant Love, looking as pink and innocent as if Purbright had just recruited him from a Dresden pastoral, and by a genial mountain whom he introduced as Sergeant Malley, the coroner's officer. The inspector arranged chairs so that while the two sergeants and the men from London faced each other, symmetry suggestive of opposing quiz teams was avoided. Then he sat down behind his desk, lit a cigarette and leaned back.

'George Tozer ... Now, then, let's hear what you know about Mr Tozer.' He blew a cloud of smoke at the ceiling.

Love and Malley glanced uncertainly at each other in-mutual suspicion of having been drawn into some absurd game.

'But … but you know old George, inspector. The barber. Down in …' Malley scowled and snapped his fingers.

'Spindle Lane,' supplied Love.

'That's it – Spindle Lane. The Rubber King.'

'You know George, sir,' insisted Love, looking at Purbright with concern.

'Of course I know him. But these gentlemen don't. And it's for their benefit I'm asking these things, not mine.'

'Oh, I see.' Malley turned his big friendly face to Pumphrey. 'He's a rum old sod, is George. Ugly as vomit. But he'd help anyone, wouldn't he, Sid?'

Love grunted confirmation.

'They reckon it was George who fixed up Lady Beryl with that third husband of hers …'

'Fourth,' corrected Love.

'Fourth, was it? Never mind. That book salesman with one ear, I mean. Everyone reckoned Lady Beryl had had it for good when her third chucked in. She'd started drinking hair restorer by then. That's how she came to know George, I suppose …'

Pumphrey, who had been nodding and making impatient noises in his throat, thrust in a question. 'What are Tozer's political affiliations?'

Malley's eyes widened. He looked round at Love, who did his best to be helpful at such short notice. 'Lady Beryl's Conservative,' he said.

Malley regarded Pumphrey once more. 'That's right, she is. Although they don't risk letting her open fêtes any more, of course. Mind you, I'm not saying George Tozer's a snob – you're Labour, perhaps, are you, sir? – well, the Labour people have done some good in their way. That's neither here nor there, though; I'm sure George wouldn't let your politics stop him doing you a good turn if he can ...'

'He's a bit of a flanneller, mind,' Love saw fit to warn Ross.

'Oh, aye,' agreed the coroner's officer. 'Reminds you of the barber's cat, doesn't he, Sid? All wind and ...' He checked himself at the sight of Pumphrey's frown of exasperation. 'Still, I'll say this for him – there's many a family in this town would be too big to be fed if it hadn't been for George's eight-penny reliables.'

Ross shifted a little in his chair. 'Perhaps we're not quite on the right tack, sergeant. Can you tell us anything about this man's associates?'

There was a short silence while Malley and Love looked at each other and then at Purbright. The inspector, however, was unhelpfully preoccupied with the tip of his cigarette.

Love scratched his head. 'I've an idea that he's in a team of bellringers ...'

'They reckon he's quite religious,' added Malley, cautiously. 'On the side, like ...'

'But I don't think he's what you might call associated with anybody specially,' wound up Love. 'I mean, why should he be?'

The hint of defiance in his voice earned a sharp stare from Pumphrey. 'The man who seems to have no associations, sergeant, is generally one who has taken good care to conceal them.'

Ross beamed a take-no-notice smile at Love. 'So much for Mr Tozer, I think. Now then, what about ... what's his name, Purbright? – the hopalong character ...'

'Crutchey Anderson.'

Malley chuckled. He winked at Pumphrey. 'You want to keep clear of that old villain; by God, you do. Don't tell me he's been asking you to teach him how to play snooker. Oh, Christ!'

Ross quickly intervened. 'It was I who came across Anderson, sergeant, not Mr Pumphrey. I'd like to know who he is, that's all.'

'Bookie's runner, that's what he is. Used to be on the shrimping boats at Chalmsbury until he put one leg into the shrimp copper when he was drunk. It was cooked to the bone before they could pull him clear. But if he thinks he can touch you for a pint, he'll give you a tale about sharks. It *is* sharks, isn't it, Sid?'

'Mostly. Except when it's frostbite at Archangel.'

'Archangel,' Ross repeated, half to himself. He looked across at the inspector. 'But tell me, Purbright, surely bookmakers don't employ runners any more. I presume Flaxborough has betting shops like everywhere else.'

'Oh, yes. But we still consider them rather *infra dig*. They look to the working classes like sub-offices of the National Assistance Board. And the middle classes seem to think they're something to do with the Co-op.'

'You mean street betting still goes on here?'

'I'm sure it does. After all, furtiveness confers a certain cachet; don't you find that, Major Ross?'

'Anderson was once a sailor, you say.' It was Pumphrey speaking now. Purbright noticed his habit of jerking his long, pointed head forward and from side to side, as if his thoughts had to be continually shaken in their box to prevent them sticking together. 'That means he could have established contacts abroad, doesn't it?'

Malley grinned indulgently. 'Abroad? If you call sand-banks two miles off the estuary abroad, I suppose he could. That's as far as the shrimpers ever go.'

'To the best of your knowledge.' By lightly stressing the 'your', Pumphrey conjured the vision of a whole fleet of small boats slipping off to dark continental anchorages while Malley slept.

'What's this fellow's style of living?' Ross asked.

Love took his turn. 'Squatter, I suppose you'd call him. One of those big Nissen huts on the old ack-ack site down Hunting's Lane. He keeps a wife at each end of it. I'm told those two have never met. That seems a bit queer, though.' He looked inquiringly at Malley.

'That's just a tale,' Malley said. 'I saw the two of them pass in Woolworth's the other day. They recognised each other, all right.'

Purbright looked at his watch. There was, he felt, a limit to the time he ought to spare from his own relatively unin-spired prosecution of the Hopjoy case. He stubbed out his cagarette. There were no more questions about Crutchey Anderson, apparently. 'That,' said Purbright, 'brings us to Mr and Mrs Croll, out at Mumblesby. All right, sergeant.'

The others looked at Malley. He stroked the back of his head, seeking suitable words in which Mrs Croll might be sketched without intemperance. He cleared his throat. 'I should say young Bernadette's had more ferret than I've had hot dinners.'

Purbright translated. 'It seems that she has something of a reputation for promiscuity.' He looked at Ross over his arched fingers. 'Do you find that to the point, Major Ross?'

It was Pumphrey who fielded the question. 'Security-wise, moral turpitude is always to the point, inspector. The ... the person in whom we are interested was following a sound principle when he put Mrs Croll under surveillance.' He spoke aside to his companion, whose expression had stiffened a good deal: 'This might be our best lead yet, you know.'

Malley gave a short laugh at the thought which had just occurred to him. 'Funny we should have been on about old Tozer a minute ago. The talk is that he used to send young blokes out to keep Bernadette company.'

'Tozer did, you say?' Ross was suddenly attentive.

'Aye. He fancies himself in the matchmaking line, you know. They say he has a list of all the lonely wives in Flax. I don't know about that, but old George is sharper than he looks; he soon finds from a customer whether he's happily married or not and how much time he spends away from home. Mind you —' Malley rubbed his chin – 'I reckon George'll think twice before he sends another stand-in for Ben Croll.'

Malley paused and patted out a crease in the front of his enormous uniform. He waited complacently.

'Why, what happened, Bill?' Purbright supplied, after an interval properly respectful to the coroner's officer.

'Well, the last one damn nearly became a client of mine. Ben turned up and caught him. He chucked him through the bedroom window like a fork-load of sugar beet. Sykes in the path lab at the General told me they had to operate the same night. The bloke was lucky to pull through.'

'What was his name?' Ross asked.

'I don't know. No one could find out. They put Trevelyan on his case sheet but that wasn't his name. Harton gave orders for the whole business to be kept quiet.'

'Harton?'

'The surgeon, Mr Ross. Sykes heard Harton tell the ward sister that it was a very special case and that no information was to be given to anybody.'

'Yes, but George Tozer would know, wouldn't he?' Love put in. 'Who the chap really was, I mean.'

'No doubt he does. And keeping it to himself. If Ben thought George had had anything to do with it, he'd run a muck-loader through his guts.'

'I might get something out of Mrs Croll,' suggested Love, hopefully.

Purbright levelled a pencil at him. 'You stay away from Mumblesby, Sid. Good God, they even go in pairs to read meters in that parish.' He turned to Malley. 'By the way, did you gather what the man's injuries actually were?'

'No, they were hushed up, too. But Harton does abdominals. Practically nothing else.'

Purbright raised his brows at Ross.

'Rassmussen,' Ross said.

'Ah, yes; Rassmussen. Anyone know who Rassmussen is?'

Love volunteered. 'He's a Dane. He used to have a farm of his own at Pollard Bridge until the Government took all that land over. I think he does odd jobs mostly nowadays. Slaughtering, for one. Some of the farmers still like to have a pig killed for their own use now and again, but not one in a hundred knows how to tackle it. So they send for Hicks here in Flaxborough – he keeps a butcher's shop – or else Rassmussen.'

'There'd be nothing unusual in Croll wanting a pig slaughtered, I suppose?' said Ross.

'What, right now, you mean, sir?'

'Yes, now.'

Love smirked. 'It's funny you should ask that. They did have one killed about a fortnight ago, but someone pinched half the carcass from where it was hanging in the barn during the night. Croll rang us up about it. He was swearing blue murder.'

'Who did that killing?'

'Hicks, I should think. I don't know, though.'

'So Croll might have sent for Rassmussen since then – having lost a big part of the first animal.'

'He might. If Hicks couldn't come the second time.'

Ross inclined his head. 'Just one other thing, sergeant. You said the Government had taken over Rassmussen's farm. How did that come about?'

The question seemed to surprise Love a little. 'Well, all the land round there was taken. Compulsory purchase, I suppose. It was for that big what d'you call it at Thimble Bay.'

Chapter Thirteen

THE NEXT DAY, assiduous Sergeant Warlock, pert and primed, stuck his head round Purbright's door and announced: 'We've done the car.'

He enumerated what suggestive finds there had been. A few fragments of straw lay on the floor of the boot – a capacious boot, Warlock agreed – and four or five bloodstains were in the same place. The straw was of a kind similar to wisps in the garage at Beatrice Avenue and in the wardrobe in the late Mrs Periam's bedroom. It was safe to assume the trail to be that of the acid carboy.

The blood was less easily explained. The stains were of recent origin but decidedly not human. 'And there you are, squire,' concluded Warlock, with the air of an energetic retriever dropping a particularly unimpressive rabbit.

Purbright stared thoughtfully at the pile of Hopjoy's belongings that still lay in a filing tray at the side of his desk. 'Tell me, sergeant: this business of bloodstains ... You can tell fairly easily whether they are human or animal, I take it.'

'Oh, rather. And the various human groups are identifiable. But only as groups, mind; we don't label individual chromosomes yet.'

'Quite. But suppose blood structure is damaged badly – destroyed, in fact. What chance would your analysis have then?'

'None, obviously.' Warlock's tone implied that he considered the question pretty wet.

'Let me put it another way. Suppose some blood, flesh, and bone were reduced right down to basic chemical constituents – carbon, water, calcium salts, and so on – is there any possible way of deciding what sort of an animal they belonged to?'

'You don't really want an answer to that, do you?'

Purbright rose and walked slowly to the window. He stood looking out, his hands clasped behind him. 'You know, this should have occurred to us before.'

Warlock's usual picture of athletic eagerness had been abandoned. He looked anxious. 'If you're thinking of the drain washings ...'

'I am, indeed.'

'Yes, well I'd better say straight away that there's no way of proving whether that sludge was man, woman, or the Archbishop of Canterbury's pet kangaroo.' He waited, then waved a hand. 'Oh, but surely to God ... I mean this bod of yours has vanished – there couldn't be a more obvious tie-up.'

'That's just what I'm afraid of.' Purbright turned. 'There are several things about this case that look a little too obvious. And you didn't imagine I'd forgotten that doctored hammer, did you?'

'That was queer, certainly. As,' Warlock added firmly, 'I pointed out.'

'You did. And I think you deserve to know something else. The presumed victim was – or is – an exceptionally fly gentleman, very hard pressed by creditors and husbands. His speciality was trading on his employment in a highly secret and I suppose romantic profession.'

'So that explains Tweedle-dum and Tweedle-dee.'

'Oh, you've met Major Ross and his colleague, have you?'

'Met them? I've practically been tried in camera by them. That one who looks like a pox-doctor's clerk – the little bloke with a sharp nose – he was bloody offensive. I told him so.' Warlock's recollection of the encounter restored his restless elasticity. He danced his weight from one foot to the other and threw a shadow punch at the wall. 'Never saw a weasel with ringworm before. Ah, well; press on.' Opening the door, he glanced back quizzically at Purbright. 'D'you really think all this was a put up job, then?'

The inspector smiled, but made no reply.

'Oh, by the way, I nearly forgot about this …' Warlock came back into the room, fishing from his breast pocket a glass tube which he tossed down on the desk. 'Fibrafon think it's from a baby's hairbrush, Portland Plastics say fishing line, and Hoffman's plump for a retaining thread in a gyro compass. Take your pick.'

Purbright recognised the nylon strand gleaned from the Beatrice Avenue plumbing. 'Not terribly helpful, are they?'

'I'll try a few more if you like. But I must say it seems a matter of asking silly questions and getting silly answers.'

The inspector put the tube aside. 'Forget about it for now. There's no point in putting your people to more trouble while there's a possibility of our having been led up a garden. Which reminds me …' – he looked up at the clock – 'that I ought to be having a word with the Chief Constable.'

*

Mr Chubb was in his greenhouse, counting out his cuttings. He looked cool and tall and grey behind the glass. Purbright closed the side gate, with its enamelled NO to hawkers, circulars and canvassers, and skirted a small crescent of lawn. The grass was littered with rubber bones, savaged tennis balls, and other no longer identifiable articles associated with the appeasement of Mr Chubb's Yorkshire terriers, whose excreta, marvellously variegated, was everywhere. The animals themselves, Purbright noted gratefully, were absent; he supposed them to be dragging a triple-leashed, panting Mrs Chubb on their daily expedition against the peace and hygiene of the neighbourhood.

The Chief Constable acknowledged Purbright's arrival with a small patient smile through the panes. The smile announced his readiness to put the public weal before petunias and duty above all delights. There clung to him as he emerged from the greenhouse the warm, aromatic redolence of tomato foliage.

Purbright was waved to a seat on a rustic bench screened by laurels from the next-door garden, where the wife of the City Surveyor could be heard scraping a burned saucepan bottom and sustaining with a periodic 'oh' or 'did she?' the muffled monotone of a kitchen visitor's narration.

Mr Chubb leaned lightly against a trellised arch and gazed into the middle distance.

'This case from Beatrice Avenue, sir,' Purbright began. 'I'd like to give you what we've gathered so far and to hear your opinion of it. Our first impressions may have been mistaken.'

'Ah …' Mr Chubb nodded almost approvingly. 'That's always to be expected, Mr Purbright. There's no discredit in finding one's calculations at fault. Seeds don't always produce what's on the packet, you know.'

'No, sir.'

Mr Chubb relinquished a few inches of his Olympian advantage and put his hand on the back of the bench. 'I'll tell you one thing, my boy. I'm very pleased that you've pegged away at this thing instead of leaving it to the heavies. Major Ross and his man are absolutely capable, I've no doubt, but outsiders never seem to understand just why people in a place like this behave as they do. It's important, you know. Very.' The assertive frown cleared and Mr Chubb's face went back aloft. 'Sorry to have interrupted. Carry on.'

'Just before I left the office' – Purbright delved into the brief case he was holding – 'I had an idea about the anonymous letter that started off this affair. You'll remember it, of course.' He handed a creased, pale blue sheet to the Chief Constable. 'And now look at this, sir: it was among the papers we found in Hopjoy's bedroom.'

Mr Chubb turned back the cover of the writing pad Purbright had taken from his case. He compared the letter with the top sheet of the pad, then smoothed one over the other. They corresponded in size, colour, and texture.

'You can follow the ball-point indentations that have come through,' Purbright pointed out. 'They persist for two or three pages down.'

'Not very anonymous now,' remarked Mr Chubb drily. He watched Purbright re-fold the letter and slip it into its parent pad. Then he frowned. 'What the dickens are we supposed to make of it all? Some sort of a joke, or what?'

'It would have been no joke for Periam if he'd been convicted of murder, sir.'

'No, by jove, it wouldn't,' murmured Mr Chubb.

'And yet,' said Purbright, 'he very well might have been. The evidence that he killed his lodger and then disposed of his body is very impressive at first sight. We get this letter and naturally presume it's from a neighbour who has heard a quarrel and might even have seen something suggestive of violence. It makes particular mention of the bathroom – a rather convincing touch, somehow. We have no choice but to investigate. And there they all are, the signs of very nasty goings on – bloodstains, wax coating on the bath, acid burns on the floor, a hammer stuck up with blood and hair. And buried in the garden, the smashed carboy, whose iron basket – too big to bury and too tough to be broken up – has been hastily pushed out of sight in a wardrobe.

'We look in the drains – quite predictably, of course – and sure enough they prove that a body has been destroyed by acid. Whose? Obviously, the loser of the midnight fight in the bathroom which was so considerately reported to us by a watchful neighbour. The winner, if and when we trace him is bound to be the murderer.

'The survivor, Gordon Periam, is duly found. He is not far away, but that fact in itself is consistent with the self-confidence of the sort of man who can commit and conceal an exceptionally horrid crime. Indeed, all the circumstances in which he is found (as you doubtless recognised yourself, sir) are classically in line. The refuge in sex relations, the flashy hotel with its novel comforts and expense, enjoyment of the victim's car as well as his girl … the pattern's complete and absolutely damning.'

The inspector paused to light a cigarette. Mr Chubb regarded him very thoughtfully. He was trying to persuade himself that the point about the classic behaviour of murderers had, indeed, already occurred to him.

'And that, sir,' resumed Purbright, 'was the situation as it was presented to us. "Presented" is the operative word, of course. It could have gone straight to the Director of Public Prosecutions there and then, and I dare say that Periam's indictment would have been automatic. But you were wise not to rush it, sir.'

The Chief Constable modestly turned his gaze to a group of border plants near his foot.

'It was almost inevitable,' Purbright went on, 'that some part of so elaborate a set-up would prove faulty. The lab people spotted it. Those hairs on the hammer were Hopjoy's all right – or at least they corresponded with some found on his clothing – but they hadn't arrived there through his having been bashed over the head. According to Warlock, they'd been snipped and stuck on.'

'Yes, but the blood ...'

'It doesn't need too much of a self-inflicted cut, possibly with the corner of a razor blade, to provide enough blood to be smeared on a hammer head. And perhaps a few splashes around the place as well.'

'There was a quarrel, though, Mr Purbright. I don't think we should let ourselves be led too far away from that fact by chaps with microscopes.'

'Oh, yes, there was a row,' Purbright agreed. 'Periam didn't deny that, as he could very well have persisted in doing. But I think I told you that he said it was a very one-sided affair, with Hopjoy doing all the shouting. If we accept that, might we not consider whether the noise had a special object – to disturb neighbours and put in their minds the presumption of a quarrel?'

'And were they disturbed?'

'Those I've spoken to myself say they heard nothing. But Sergeant Love is making inquiries in the houses that back on to Beatrice Avenue. The people there are far more likely to have heard whatever there was to hear; the sound would travel straight across the gardens.'

The Chief Constable nodded. 'All right. Now about this business of the body – how do you explain that away? The stuff in the drains and all that.'

'Have you ever read anything about cannibalism, sir?'

'Not avidly, Mr Purbright, no.'

'Well, it seems that human flesh quite closely resembles pork.'

'Indeed.'

'And I learned more or less by chance yesterday that half a pig carcass was stolen recently from a farm where Hopjoy had been a regular and quite intimate visitor. In the boot of that car of his, and in one or two places at the house, Warlock turned up traces of animal blood.'

For nearly a minute, Mr Chubb silently regarded an earwig's progress along one of the trellis spars.

'I suppose we have to remember,' he said at last, 'that tomfoolery of that kind was just the fellow's line of country. It's perfectly disgraceful, though, when you think of all the money that's being spent on the intelligence service. The trouble is, they live in a world of their own. I can't see that there's anything we can do about him. I mean there's nothing we can charge him with.'

Purbright pursed his lips. 'Conduct likely to lead ...'

'... to a breach of the peace?' Mr Chubb capped the phrase with a sort of sad derision. 'You can see his people letting us go ahead with that one, can't you? Worse than the blasted Diplomatic Corps. He'll turn up somewhere else with a cock and bull story and start working up a new set of creditors, just you see.'

'There's rather more to this,' said Purbright slowly, 'than mere debt-dodging. A man can arrange his own disappearance without leaving somebody else to face a murder charge. In this case, a great deal of trouble and ingenuity was spent specifically on the incrimination of Periam. But the only thing poor old Periam wasn't carefully provided with was a motive. Why should he have wanted to kill Hopjoy? If anyone had a motive for murder it was Hopjoy himself – the man whose girl Periam had appropriated.'

Mr Chubb considered. 'I see your point. But surely Hopjoy was a bit of a blackguard where women were concerned. Would he have been all that upset about one in particular?'

'Promiscuity and jealousy are by no means incompatible, sir.'

The Chief Constable raised his brows.

'In fact, the more sexually adventurous a man is, the more violently he tends to resent trespass on his own preserves.'

'Oh,' said Mr Chubb, meekly. 'You think then ...' – he turned to see where the earwig had got to – 'we should be wrong to let the whole thing drop?'

Purbright rose. 'I quite agree with you, sir; we should keep an eye on things a little longer. Hopjoy certainly ought to be traced, even if Major Ross tries to go against your judgement.'

Mr Chubb resolutely picked the earwig from the trellis and trod on it.

'After all,' said Purbright, 'there has been, in a sense, one attempt on Periam's life. When it is seen to have failed, there may be another – on less unorthodox lines.'

Chapter Fourteen

TO THE MULTITUDE of elusives for whom watch is proclaimed to be kept at British ports, rail termini, and airports, was added the name of Brian Hopjoy. If encountered, he was to be asked simply to get into touch with the Chief Constable of Flaxborough. The request had been difficult to frame. 'What do we say we want him for?' Mr Chubb had asked; '... to collect his hat?' He had carefully refrained from mentioning the matter to Ross or Pumphrey, although he did ask, at Purbright's suggestion, if he might borrow from them the photograph of Hopjoy which, as far as anyone could find out, was the only one in existence. Pumphrey, looking as if he had been casually requested to assassinate the Prime Minister when he next happened to be in London, had emphasised with some asperity the topness of the secrecy involved and begged him to be more circumspect.

The withholding of the photograph made local inquiries more difficult, too. Purbright prepared a composite of descriptions offered by the next-door neighbours, Mr Tozer, and the manager of the Neptune Hotel – who seemed especially eager to help – and gave it to the two plain clothes men who could be spared for visits to railway stations and bus depots and taxi firms within a radius of three or four miles. The usual feats of memory were forthcoming: Hopjoys had entrained for London, Birmingham, and Newcastle simultaneously with their journeys by road to Lincoln, Cambridge, Swindon, and Keswick.

Sergeant Love, conscientiously but fruitlessly urging the residents of Pawson's Lane to recall sounds of angry altercation in a house 'over the back', found time to present the inspector with a theory he had evolved on his own.

'This chap was in hospital fairly recently, according to Bill Malley, wasn't he?'

'He was. A lover's tiff, I gather – with the husband.'

'Yes, well if it was something serious he might still need treatment. You know – you hear of fellows on the run who have to nip into a doctor's when they use up their special pills.'

'That field's a bit narrow, Sid. We should have heard if Hopjoy were a diabetic, surely. Still, it's worth a try; that description badly needs strengthening, if only with a scar or two.'

The sergeant, one of whose private dreams accommodated Editor Love, waistcoated and dynamic, appraising a re-plated page one, set off again for Pawson's Lane with his mind embannered by SCARFACED PLAYBOY SOUGHT IN WARD TEN: MUST RENEW MIRACLE DRUG.

*

No such dramatic and socially desirable potentialities appeared to have occurred to Sister Howell, in charge of the male surgical ward at Flaxborough General Hospital. She was a cool, smooth, stiffly laundered woman, with an indestructible smile guarding the pink sugar fortress of her face while her eyes were absent on their continual darting quest for faults. Purbright delivered his inquiry with the sense of being accounted no more important than one of the dust motes that submissively descended through a shaft of sunlight to the level of Sister Howell's sensible shoes.

She heard him out. Then she slightly re-arranged the smile (the eyes still could not be spared, even for the briefest introduction) and told him that much as she would like to be obliging, he would, of course, understand that it was quite, quite impossible to divulge confidential medical matters even to an inspector of police.

Purbright assured her that he did appreciate and respect her loyalty, but wondered if perhaps she could modify it in the wider interests of justice. It had, unhappily, become the task of the police to trace her former patient, who had disappeared, and knowledge of his late injuries or ailments might be of considerable assistance.

'I'm sorry,' said Sister Howell, folding fingers devotionally over her apron.

'Then perhaps if I were to refer to Mr Harton personally …'

The eyes, instantly obedient to recall in appropriate circumstances, were trained upon him at last. 'Mr Harton is a very busy man. He's probably in theatre. I really couldn't …'

The door at the end of the corridor swung open abruptly. A procession bore down upon them. Sister Howell plucked Purbright's sleeve and drew him against the wall. 'There's Mr Harton now,' she whispered urgently. Purbright wondered if he were expected to kneel.

The surgeon advanced with a slow, easy stroll. Keeping precisely level with him were the short, sturdy legs of the Matron, to the rhythm of whose ponderous trot her cassock-red dewlap rose and fell. Harton and his consort were closely followed by a young nurse who carried a stack of folders and gazed idolatrously at the back of the surgeon's head. Then came a pair of house physicians in white coats, unbuttoned and trailing black tentacles from the pockets. Seven or eight students, murmuring to one another and looking at their hands, shuffled along in the rear. Every now and again the parade was halted while Mr Harton paid particular, head-inclined attention to the Matron's commentary and rewarded her with a mellifluent ring of laughter.

As the procession was about to wheel off into the ward, Purbright politely but firmly removed Sister Howell's restraining hand and stepped forward. He smiled apologetically at the Matron, then introduced himself to Harton. The surgeon, imperturbably gracious, took him aside into the empty duty room. Through the closed glass door Purbright saw the retinue congeal into attitudes of respectful patience.

Harton, whom Purbright had thought it politic to give fairly fully the reasons for his inquiry, nodded with good-humoured sagacity. Nearly as tall as the policeman, he had skin the colour of an advertisement for tinned ham. This slightly incredible wholesomeness of complexion was emphasised (quite horridly, some thought) by strong, disciplined waves of prematurely white hair. His were the bright, steady eyes of one who has learned to render charm intimidating. The flawless cheeks flanked an unexpectedly tiny, drawn-in mouth, his only unrelaxed feature, which ambition had prinked like a flan edging. When he spoke, which he did most musically, his lower teeth were displayed more than the upper.

'My dear inspector …' – he felt behind him for the table and leaned against it with some of his weight supported upon spread fingertips – 'you mustn't take all this medical etiquette too seriously. It's designed to give our dear old girls something to occupy them.' He grinned boyishly through the window at the Matron.

'So you've no objection to giving me this information, sir?'

'None whatsoever.'

Purbright waited, but Harton merely continued to regard him placidly.

'Well, sir …?'

'Well, inspector?'

'You were about to tell me the nature of the operation you performed upon Mr Trevelyan.'

'Oh, no; that is not so.'

Purbright stared. 'Perhaps we've misunderstood each other, sir.'

'Ah, possibly we have. What I said was that I, I personally, you understand, have no objection to telling you what you wish to know. That is quite true. But I did not say that no objection existed, did I?'

The inspector sighed. Here, he reflected, was the type of man who would enjoy confusing shop assistants with pedantic pleasantries.

'The fact is, inspector' – Harton thrust a hand deep into his trousers' pocket and energetically stirred some coins – 'that I simply am not at liberty to follow my personal inclination to tell you what was the matter with our mutual friend.'

'Oh, you do know, then, sir?'

Harton smiled away the calculated impertinence. 'Certainly I know. Surgeons do occasionally remember what they have done and why. In their own way they are possibly as methodical as policemen.'

'I suppose that what you really mean to say, sir, is that you have received instructions to divulge nothing concerning Mr Trevelyan's stay in hospital?'

'I must say I do not much care for the word "instructions" but, roughly speaking, that is the position, inspector. Dare I whisper that old cliché "national security"?' Elegantly, Harton drew himself erect and stepped to the door. 'Incidentally, we found Mr Trevelyan a most charming fellow; I do hope your anxiety regarding him proves to have been groundless.'

Placing a hand lightly on Purbright's shoulder, he opened the door with the other. 'I am sure it will, you know.' He patted him out and jauntily gestured the procession to re-form.

*

Purbright drove at once to Brockleston.

Among the cars in the Neptune forecourt was Hopjoy's Armstrong, which he had ordered to be placed again at the disposal of Mr and Mrs Periam. The honeymooners he found playing clock golf in the hotel grounds. Doreen, her coiled plaits looking like some kind of protective sporting gear, wore a long pink cardigan over a flowered dress. Her husband was in flannel trousers and the dark brown blazer of the Flaxborough Grammar School Old Boys' Association.

When he saw the inspector, he picked up his ball and led the girl forward. 'Has Brian shown up yet?'

'I'm afraid not, Mr Periam.'

'Oh. We thought that's what you'd come to tell us.' The solemn, femininely smooth face turned to the girl. 'Didn't we, darl?'

Periam grouped three of the bright canvas chairs at the edge of the putting green. They sat.

'No, Mr Hopjoy has not returned. I rather doubt if he will. But I think it's only right for me to relieve your minds on one point.' Purbright glanced from one to the other. 'It now looks as though we were mistaken in assuming that your friend was dead.'

Doreen seized her husband's hand. 'There! What did I say?' At Purbright she pouted in mock indignation. 'And fancy chasing us with that ridiculous story when we hadn't been married five minutes? It wasn't what I'd call tactful.'

'It wasn't, Mrs Periam. I'm sorry. But in the circumstances we hadn't much choice.'

Periam looked at the handle of the putter he had laid across his knee. 'That's all right, inspector. It hasn't been very nice for us – I mean we should have felt rather responsible if anything awful *had* happened to Bry – we did let him down, you know, darl – but the police couldn't be blamed for that.' He raised his head and smiled wryly at Purbright. 'Now you know what sort of capers you ask for when you run off with your best friend's young lady.'

Doreen sighed and pressed Periam's hand to her stomach. Hastily he withdrew it. 'Oh, there's one thing, inspector ... the house. You have finished there, haven't you? You see, we ...'

'If you can wait just a couple of days, sir, everything will be put straight again. We'll see to that for you, naturally.'

'And thanks for letting us have the car back.'

'Was it covered in blood and fingerprints?'

Periam cast a quick glance of rebuke at his wife. 'Doreen, really …'

'I suppose,' Purbright said, 'that you'll settle down in the house when your holiday's over. Or are you thinking of a change now you're married?'

'No, we shan't move. Not yet, anyway. It's been home for so long, you know, and I am rather a home bird. Anyway, I'm sure mother wouldn't have wished strangers to take it over.'

'I expect you know there are various odds and ends belonging to Mr Hopjoy. We'd rather like to hang on to them for the time being, but if you do hear from him perhaps you'll let us have a forwarding address; would you mind doing that, sir?'

'Not at all.'

'There's one other matter I'm mildly curious about, Mr Periam. A short while ago Mr Hopjoy was in hospital. I believe I know the circumstances in which he was injured – we needn't go into them now – but I wondered if you could tell me what his injuries actually were.'

Periam ran a finger thoughtfully round his heavy, globular chin. 'Well, not in doctor's parlance, I can't. But he had what I'd call a gammy foot.'

'How serious was it? I mean was there any permanent effect – scars, disfigurements, anything of that sort?'

'My goodness, no. He came home right as rain. Between you and I, I think old Bry had been coming the old soldier in hospital. He'd probably been giving the glad-eye to some pretty nurse.'

'He wasn't disabled in any sense, then?'

'Not a bit of it, inspector. It would take more than a tumble to put Bry out of action, wouldn't it, Darl?'

'Rather,' agreed Doreen. She had coyly abstracted a packet of biscuits from Periam's pocket and was nibbling one after having prised it open to inspect its filling.

'He's as strong as a horse,' Periam went on. The theme seemed to intrigue him. 'I shouldn't care to tangle with Bry when he'd got his dander up.' Purbright reflected that Hopjoy must have been sadly off form on the occasion of his tangling with Farmer Croll. Or was it in the matter of danders that Croll had enjoyed a decisive advantage?

Periam grasped his putter and looked inquiringly at the inspector.

Purbright rose. 'I don't think I need interrupt your game any longer. I'm sorry if I've been something of a ...' He faltered, suddenly averse to making even conventional apology.

'... a skeleton at the feast?' suggested Periam, almost jocularly.

'Oh, but such a nice skeleton!' Purbright had the brief but disconcerting sensation of Doreen's bosom being nuzzled roguishly against his arm. Then she was walking away and looking back at him over her shoulder as she munched another of Periam's biscuits.

*

Sergeant Malley breathed hard but contentedly between puffs at a pipe in which seemed to be smouldering a compound of old cinema carpet and tar. He sat in the windowless little office in the police station basement where witnesses at forthcoming inquests were induced by the huge sergeant's calm and kindness to give more or less lucid expression to their recollections of tragedy.

Malley, whom even inspectors and superintendents treated as host in his own confined quarters – if only because they could not bear to see him trying to uncork eighteen stone from an inadequate chair – listened without surprise to Purbright's account of his call at the hospital.

'I could have told you that you'd be wasting your time. Harton's about as obliging as an empty stamp machine. And those bloody women ...' He shook his head.

'Look, Bill, I've no objection to these people playing at guess-what-God's-up-to if that makes them happy. But I'd still like to find the character who started all this phoney MI Fivemanship.'

Malley wriggled forward a few inches and folded his arms on the desk. 'If you're really interested in that operation, I think I might be able to find you someone who'll talk. He's one of the theatre assistants and a pal of Jack Sykes – the bloke in the lab I was telling you about. Do you want me to have a go?'

'I wish you would. It may not be important, of course; Periam said Hopjoy just hurt his leg slightly and carried no sign, but I suppose he can't know for certain.'

'Hurt his leg?'

'That's right.'

'But Harton doesn't do legs. He's an innards man.'

'Oh.' Purbright considered. 'Yes, you said something about that before. Then perhaps Hopjoy was just spinning Periam one of his celebrated tales.'

'Maybe.'

'I wonder why ... Never mind – let me know if you get hold of Mr Sykes's friend, won't you.'

A face, thrust inquisitively into the narrow doorway, creased with nausea on encountering Sergeant Malley's pipe fumes. 'Christ!' said Sergeant Love, adding 'sir' when he discerned the inspector through the haze.

Purbright joined him in the corridor.

'I've gone right through the people in Pawson's Lane, sir. And guess what?' Love's eye glistened with something more than reaction to smoke.

'No, you tell me, Sid.' The inspector put a paternal arm round his shoulder.

'I've found the woman who wrote that anonymous letter.'

Purbright stared at him. 'What anonymous letter?'

'The one we got about the do at Periam's place. You know, sir. The thing that started all this.'

Chapter Fifteen

'MY DEAR SIDNEY, we know all about that letter. It wasn't written by a neighbour. Hopjoy wrote it himself.'

Love shook his head. 'I'm afraid I'm not with you, sir.'

'I said Hopjoy wrote it. He wasn't terribly subtle; a pad of the same paper was among the stuff in his bedroom.'

Love grudgingly digested the information. 'Well, all I can say is that there must have been two, and that the Cork woman's got lost. It was one of the first things she said. "I feel rather bad about sending that letter," she said. "I didn't mean to cause trouble." I told her not to worry about it because it hadn't really made any difference and anyway she hadn't put her name to it, then she cheered up a bit and said something about it being the least she could have done for the poor boy's mother. I think,' Love added by way of explanation, 'that she's a bit clobby in the cockpit.'

'There are two women there; which one are you talking about?'

'The daughter. There wasn't a squeak out of Ma. She just hovered.'

'You asked about the row in the bathroom?'

'Yes. She said she didn't hear shouting or anything like that although she'd been watching the window while the light was on.'

'But if she was awake, surely she must have heard something. There's not thirty yards between those houses. And even Periam admitted Hopjoy was yelling his head off. He of all people had nothing to gain by making that up: very much the reverse. Anyway, if there was no disturbance why the devil should she have taken it into her head to send off this letter she talks about?'

Love remained silent for a few seconds. Then, as if trying to compensate for some lapse of his own, he said: 'Mind you, she did say she thought she heard a noise like breaking glass later on when she'd gone to bed. That could have been the acid thing, couldn't it? And she said she got up again and saw somebody moving about in the garden.'

'I rather think,' Purbright said, 'that I should have a word with Miss Cork myself. In the meantime, Sid ...' – he drew from his pocket an envelope – 'I wonder if you'd mind hawking this lighter around Hopjoy's acquaintances to see if they can identify it.'

Contrary to Purbright's expectations, the Corks received him with something approaching affability. The daughter led him to a parlour with the temperature of an orchid house – a small but fierce fire burned in the scrupulously tidy grate – and went off to make tea. Mrs Cork greeted him with a slow inclination of the head. She sat in a tapestried chair in the window bay. While her daughter was out of the room, she said nothing but stared at him approvingly, nodding from time to time as if she were half afraid that he might, if not thus encouraged, take himself off before the kettle boiled.

Purbright looked about him at a room that he supposed its owners would describe as a treasure chest of memories. Scarcely a single feature of its clustered contents had the look of ever being put to use. Books in a glass-fronted cabinet had been pushed into obscurity to make shelf room for ornate china cruets, an old calendar, dusty oddments of barbola work and a collection of cards from bygone Christmases. Vases, of which there was a great number, were dry and flowerless, although a spray of paper roses emerged lopsidedly from a biscuit barrel. Within a set of three square decanters were the pale ochre stains of ancient sediment. An alabaster ashtray, bearing a card suit indicator, was lodged with a box of counters, a china boot and a manicure set, inside a cut glass salad bowl.

Pictures blockaded the room. Their flagships, so to speak, were a heavily framed lithograph depicting a horse thrusting its head through an open cottage window during the family meal ('An Unbidden Guest') and an enormous tinted engraving of Windsor Castle with besashed and garlanded picknickers in the foreground. A dozen or so photographs, standing on pieces of furniture or suspended on long cords from the picture rail, projected the sad, sepia stares of dead relations, trussed for their appointments with posterity by studio palm or rustic bridge.

The room smelled of linoleum and passed-down sewing boxes. There hung also upon the over-heated air the faintly mothballish odour of female old age.

Miriam Cork prepared the three cups of tea with finicky expertise on a tray balanced on her lap. Pouring tea, the inspector noticed, was an occupation that gave this stringy, straight-backed woman a kind of fulfilment. Her thin mouth was set in concentration. The big nose with a wart on its side seemed to stretch forth in anxious assessment of the strength and fragrance of the brew. Her eyes, pale and uncalm with hypochondria, steadied to measure the mounting amber line; there even shone in them a little pride.

Purbright began his questions. They invoked the sort of loquacity of which only that woman is capable who receives confidences from God in proportion to her readiness to interest herself in the frailties of mankind.

Oh, yes, she had known the Periam family ever since Gordon was a little mite. He had been a blessing to his mother, poor soul, whom God in His wisdom had sent widowhood through the agency of a brewer's van with a loose wheel. Right through the years he had maintained his devotion to her – in spite of everything a certain brazen Miss Come-and-get-me had been able to do to take him away and have him marry her.

'He had a girlfriend in those days, had he?' Purbright found the notion intriguing.

'If that's what you can call her. She was hanging round him ever since he was at school. But he didn't let his mother be worried. That girl never stepped over the doorstep until after Mrs Periam was in her coffin. Of course, I knew when the end was coming, and it wasn't just because I'd heard about the operation. It was a terrible operation, mind; they took all her insides away. No, the day before she passed on I saw my man in the black overcoat walk slowly by the window there. And I said straight away to mother, "Mother, Mrs Periam's going: that man's been by again".'

Mrs Cork, gazing out of the window with rheumy, unseeing eyes, gave a tired nod of corroboration.

'It was just the same with Uncle Will. And with old Mr Elliott at the corner. Each time I saw the man in the overcoat. I always know when blinds are going to be drawn.'

Association of ideas prompted Purbright to interrupt with: 'That night the sergeant was asking you about, Miss Cork ... tell me just what you saw across the way.'

She switched without the slightest hesitation to the new line of reminiscence. 'It was one of my bad nights' – two bony fingers stole gently to explore the neighbourhood of her solar plexus. 'The doctors warned me never to take anything with pips for fear they might lodge, and that teatime I'd had just half a fig roll, no more, but it was enough; I was in agony until first light and then the paraffin started working, thank the Lord – I did thank Him, too – right there on the what-have-you and I wasn't ashamed to. But didn't Dr Harris give me what for the next day when I told him. "Mirrie," he said – he always calls me Mirrie – "what did I tell you about pips? I said if one lodges after what you've gone through, it's a box for you, my girl." Well, he was smiling, of course, but you could see how worried he really was; he was quite white round the mouth ...'

'You were sleepless, Miss Cork: I'd gathered that much from Sergeant Love. Now what did you hear and see at Mr Periam's house?'

'Well, the bathroom light was on for one thing. Oh, for ages. I thought they'd gone to bed and forgotten it. But then the dining-room light came on. It was quite late – past midnight – but once I get one of those turns it's no use trying to get to sleep ...'

'Did you see anyone in the dining-room?'

'No, the curtains were drawn. And of course the bathroom window is that ripply stuff. You can see shapes through it, but not to make them out very clearly. I mean you can tell if anyone's going to have a bath because the shape's pink. Then, naturally, you stop looking. But that night there was no need not to look. There was only Mr Hopjoy washing – he never even takes his shirt off for that – and then a bit later Mr Periam doing his exercises.'

'Exercises?'

'Yes, he has one of those chest expander things. Mind, he shows for it, too: Mr Hopjoy's a poor stick beside him.'

'And that's all you saw, Miss Cork?'

'That's all. I went back for a lie-down a bit later when the pains were getting too much for me. They were just easing off after about an hour when there was that breaking noise. I couldn't be sure, but it sounded like glass – muffled, though. I got up and looked out again. This time the only light I could see was round the side; I think it must have been the garage. Then somebody came out into the garden.'

'Could you make out who it was?'

She shook her head. 'It was really just a dark shape moving about, a sort of shadow.'

'What happened after that?'

The woman looked thoughtfully into her teacup. 'Nothing, really ... Oh, except that a light did go on for a few seconds in Mrs Periam's bedroom – what used to be her bedroom, I mean, though Gordon's kept it exactly as it was, you know. Whoever went in must have pulled the curtains first; they were closed when the light was switched on.'

'You can't think of anything else?'

'Not that night, no.'

'On another, then.'

She was silent for a moment. 'I might have been imagining.'

'Never mind. Tell me about it.'

'Well, it was three or four nights later; I can't remember exactly. I'd been downstairs for some Thermogene and was dozing off again when I heard water running. It made just the sort of gurgle that the Periam's waste pipe always makes. But I'd seen no one about there for a few days, so I thought perhaps it came from one of the other houses. I didn't think about it again until that day we saw some policemen messing about with the drains.'

Of course, Purbright told himself, the bath would have had to be emptied after the day or two needed to dissolve its occupant – or half occupant. He had not got round to giving the point much thought. Yet it would have been simple enough for Hopjoy either to have lain low in the house or to have made a quiet return visit at night for long enough to pull a plug. There was another matter he found much more puzzling.

'Tell me, Miss Cork,' he said slowly, 'why these apparently insignificant things impressed you so deeply that you thought it your duty to send an anonymous letter.' He saw the look of surprise and alram in the woman's face and held up his hand. 'No, don't worry – there's no question of your getting into any sort of trouble. As a matter of fact,' he added, 'I haven't even seen it.'

'But of course you haven't seen it. It wasn't sent to you. And anyway it had nothing to do with what I've been telling you. Had it, mother?' In her perplexity, Miriam made her first acknowledgement of the old woman's silent presence.

Mrs Cork stared stonily at the inspector, then gave a stern little shake of her head.

Purbright frowned. 'I don't think I quite understand, Miss Cork. It was you who mentioned the letter in the first place to my sergeant. We assumed ...'

'Oh, no. There's been some mistake. I don't think I want to talk about it. Not about *that*, I mean. I couldn't.' Miss Cork's sparsely fleshed features registered a mixture of righteousness and disgust.

'The letter was about something you saw?' Purbright gently persisted.

'Naturally.' Her lips closed again primly.

'At the house over the back?'

She nodded. Her expression guided Purbright's next guess. 'There were ...' he paused delicately, '... goings on?'

The woman turned and stared icily at the fire, as though willing it to go out.

Either Periam's confession of disloyalty, reflected Purbright, had been a masterly understatement or else Miriam Cork possessed sensitivity remarkable even in a middle-aged spinster. He probed further.

'In a bedroom, I presume?'

Like the slow striking of a match came her reply. 'On Mrs Periam's bed.' There was a long pause. 'Romping like dogs on a grave.' Another pause. 'In the middle of the afternoon.'

'The girl ... her name was Doreen: am I right?'

Miss Cork raised her eyes from the obstinately still burning fire and directed them at a big pair of binoculars that kept a Bible text propped against the wall above the mantelpiece. 'Doreen Mackenzie,' she said, in a voice deliberately drained of tone.

'I see ... Well, we needn't dwell on that. Now this letter – I suppose you sent it to her fiancé?'

Again Miss Cork offered no immediate reply. Her hand crept once more to the centre of her ordeal by fig roll. 'I've had this out in prayer,' she announced finally, 'and I was told that I had taken the right road. The answer to your question is yes, if you feel it will do you any good. But I don't want to talk about it any more.'

The inspector, taking her at her word, departed gracefully and not without satisfaction. Something which had puzzled him considerably was now clear.

The decision to encompass a man's destruction by convincingly attributing a murder to him required very powerful provocation.

And the sort of revelations Miss Cork seemed capable of penning to a betrayed lover would provide, Purbright now felt sure, just that.

Chapter Sixteen

CHARLES FAWBY, CHIEF reporter of the *Brockleston Shuttle* and district correspondent for evening papers at Nottingham, Leicester, and Lincoln and of all the national mornings as well, would have been the first to admit that his district was less productive of hard news than most. Its houses never burned down; no gunman had ever sought a share of the small turnover of Brockleston's two branch banks; the hotel registers remained innocent of the aliases of adulterous celebrities; even the beach was lamentably safe.

And yet Brockleston-rooted stories flowered in the Press as persistently as daisies in a city lawn.

Like daisies, they were small. They appeared always at page bottoms. Fawby did not mind that. A guinea for a three-line drollery represented a much more satisfactory return for labour than ten pounds or so for a page lead that might take the best part of a day to work upon and half the evening to telephone to morose, sceptical, and hostile copy-takers.

He knew exactly what would tickle a sub-editor's fancy and help meet the insatiable demand for short 'fills'. His remunerative gleanings ranged from scraps of unconscious humour in the officialese of the district council minutes to whimsical remarks by old gentlemen arraigned in the local magistrates' courts for drunkenness. Quips, parochial paradoxes, providential puns on street names, ironic errors, quaint coincidences: all these fed Fawby's paragraphs.

What even this perceptive and adroit young man could never have foreseen, though, was that one of his modest guinea-earners was destined to confound an inspector of police, snap a chain of singularly plausible but false evidence and reveal a murderer.

The piece appeared at the foot of the fourth column on page one of the county evening having the largest sale in Flaxborough. It was headed SALT PORK, and ran, in Mr Fawby's admirably pithy prose: 'The season's oddest catch was landed at Brockleston South jetty this morning by a Sheffield angler. It was half a pig, rather the worse for immersion. And the name of the fisherman? Mr Andrew Hogg.'

Purbright stared at the page as though he had spotted his own obituary. Then he rang for Sergeant Love. There was no reply from the CID room. Purbright remembered that Love was touting a cigarette lighter round the friends of the late Hopjoy.

The late ... He realised with a start that the words had sprung quite spontaneously into his mind. Had he, despite the credit he had so readily accorded Hopjoy as an ingenious schemer, known all along that ...

He read the paragraph again, and sighed. Coincidence in the matter of such relative rarities as wandering sides of pork was too much to hope for. And Brockleston, of all places ... of course, the sea was precisely the sort of dumping ground that would have occurred to a man returning in a hurry to his seaside hotel and anxious to dispose of a murder prop that had served its turn. Even if the carcass were to wash up again, there was scarcely any possibility of its coming to the notice of a police force twelve miles away.

Purbright rose abruptly from his desk and walked to the window. It was seldom that he felt annoyed with himself – or anyone else, for that matter – but now he experienced a strong temptation to punch a hole in the glass. There was something – some unwarrantable assumption or piece of credulity on his part – which had turned this whole case the wrong way round almost from the beginning. What the hell was it?

Hands in pockets, he prowled to the door, round his desk, again to the window. He thought back over a dozen interviews, peering again at faces and listening to voices in the hope of catching some hint of what had led him so hopelessly astray. The impression grew that a single cardinal error was responsible – his swallowing without question of a whopping lie. He concentrated on recalling the occasion most likely to have produced large lies – his first meeting with Gordon Periam.

And with Mrs Periam, Doreen. Doreen Mackenzie. The erstwhile 'young lady' of Brian Hopjoy, the girl whose sportive tendencies in mid-afternoon had so shocked observant Miss Cork ...

Suddenly Purbright turned from the window. He snatched from his desk a large envelope that awaited posting to Periam and tore it open. He sought hastily among its contents for a letter in the spidery handwriting of a condoling aunt, glanced through it and made for the door.

*

This time, Miss Cork did not ask her visitor in. She remained standing just inside the porch and looked at

Purbright as if she had never seen him before. After only the tersest preamble, he launched from the doorstep the one question he had come to ask.

'Miss Cork, when you told me of writing a letter to Miss Mackenzie's fiancé, did you mean Mr Hopjoy?'

She stared as she might at a detergent promoter who had gabbled an idiotic jingle and awaited some prescribed and equally inane response before handing her a pound.

'This is most important, Miss Cork. Was it Mr Hopjoy to whom you wrote that letter?'

'I don't know what you mean. No, of course it wasn't Mr Hopjoy. I wouldn't' – the thin frame stiffened – 'soil paper with that man's name. It was Mr Periam she was engaged to. And had been for four years.'

'So it was Hopjoy with whom she ... whom you saw ...'

For a moment the woman's eyes closed. The big nose twitched in confirmation of the unspeakable.

Purbright half turned, ready to leave. 'I'm sorry if I've seemed rather stupid about this; I just wanted to make sure there was no misunderstanding.'

Miss Cork breathed with the slow self-control of the determinedly delicate. 'But I really don't see what there can have been to misunderstand. I told you that ... that *girl* – a twisted mouthing of the one word tumbled Miss Mackenzie into a broth pot of precocious lust – 'had been after poor Gordon practically since they were children.'

Purbright fingered the letter in his pocket. 'As a point of interest, do you happen to know if Doreen Mackenzie ever had a nickname?'

'I know what they called her at the Sunday school. Probably other people called her it, too. Mackie. Sometimes just Mack.'

*

Once all the little elements of truth began, as it seemed, to surrender themselves, Purbright found their marshalling together into a whole and obvious exposition of what really had happened at Beatrice Avenue quite exhilarating.

Sensing the inspector's mood, Sergeant Malley beamed avuncularly as he ushered in his hospital informant, friend of a friend, and as anxious to meet the obligations implied by that compelling relationship as he was, in his own phrase, 'to do that supercilious bastard Harton one in the eye.'

Male nurse Peter Tewkes was a curly-haired, florid, and robust young man whom impudent good nature had made popular with patients and, in axiomatic consequence, the despair of his superiors. He eyed Purbright approvingly, as if cataloguing him as an ambulant case, no bed pans or blanket baths, maybe beer in locker and good for a fourth at solo after night sister's round. 'Fire away, sir,' he invited.

'It was very good of you, Mr Tewkes, to come along and help us. I need hardly tell you that we are not seeking this information out of idle curiosity.'

Mr Tewkes raised his brow. What better motive, he seemed to ask, could there possibly be?

'You'll remember a patient being admitted under the name of Trevelyan – Howard Trevelyan, I believe.'

'I remember him,' said Tewkes, 'but I don't think that was his real name.'

'Nor do I, but never mind. He'd had a fall, hadn't he?

'So we were told. That fitted his injuries anyway.'

'Ah,' Purbright said, 'now those are what we should like to hear about. Can you oblige, Mr Tewkes?'

Tewkes gave a wide, easy shrug. 'Why not? He had a ruptured liver, that's what.'

'I see. And that made an operation necessary?'

'Oh, rather. Straight away. It's a rather nasty thing, you know.'

'I imagine it is. And the operation itself – is it very drastic?'

'I don't know that I'd call it that, exactly. The idea is simply to mend the thing, as you would a ... well, a torn cushion, say. Sew it up.' Tewkes paused. 'Mind you, I don't mean to suggest the business is particularly easy or straightforward. The biggest snag ... I say, you don't want a lot of technical stuff, do you?'

'Not if you can avoid it.'

'Right you are. I'm not awfully strong on jargon, anyway. The point is that livers don't mend themselves like most other bits of insides, so the artificial repairs have to be permanent – that's why they use non-soluble sutures – and they've got to be treated with a good deal of respect ever after.'

'I follow. Now I've been told that this man came out of hospital in reasonably frisky condition. Is that likely, in your opinion? Would he have been able to ... well, to lift heavy weights, for instance?'

Tewkes grinned. 'The only thing he'll be lifting for a bit will be a glass, and he'd better not make too regular a habit of that, either.'

'I don't fancy he will,' said Purbright soberly. He remained thinking awhile, then pulled open a drawer of the desk.

'You mentioned just now something you called non-soluble sutures. Would they be made of nylon?'

'I believe they are, as a rule, yes.'

'Have a look at that, will you?' The inspector placed before Tewkes the small glass tube bequeathed by Sergeant Warlock.

Tewkes held the tube to the light and squinted at the fine, yellowish-white strand it contained. 'Could be, certainly. Where did you get it?'

Purbright was so pleased with Mr Tewkes that he nearly rewarded him there and then with a true and full answer. Deciding after all that really wouldn't do, he said simply: 'It was stuck in a drainpipe.'

Tewkes wrinkled up one eye. 'Stuck in a ...'

Purbright nodded.

'But how bloody queer!' Tewkes gazed again at the tube, turning it this way and that in his big hands. He looked up and smiled. 'Go on – I'll buy it.'

Purbright returned his grin, a little apologetically, and reached for the tube. 'Sorry. The price is too high, Mr Tewkes. Far too high.'

Chapter Seventeen

'BUT THE LOUNGE, sergeant ... the lounge! he can't be left in the lounge!'

Sergeant Love, who was feeling by no means happy himself, found the distraught manager of the Neptune increasingly hard to bear.

'Now look, Mr Barraclough, I regret this as much as you do – perhaps more, because I feel a bit to blame – but what's done is done. The inspector will be here very soon and he'll make all the decisions. In the meantime everything must be left exactly as it is.'

'But it's nearly six o'clock.'

'What's that got to do with it?'

Mr Barraclough, in his agitation, nearly retorted: 'Opening time, of course,' but he just managed a more seemly formula. 'Six is the licensed hour for non-residents.'

Love was unmoved. 'That doesn't matter. I've locked the door. Nobody's going to get a fright.'

He sat down in a chair near the lift. From it he commanded views both of the receptionist – of her upper parts, anyway; for the moment Love found sufficient the mere memory of his earlier glimpse of those portions he had appraised, after his first surprise as 'snazzy' – and of the main hotel entrance.

Through that entrance at exactly a quarter past six walked Inspector Purbright, Major Ross, Pumphrey, and the county police surgeon. Behind them, an ambulance drew across the forecourt in a half circle and backed somewhere out of Love's line of vision.

The sergeant rose and hurried up to Purbright. His face had lost a good deal of its usual expression of luminous equanimity. Purbright gave him a concerned glance. 'Don't look so woebegone, Sid; they don't charge you just for being here.'

'I'm ever so sorry, sir, honestly …'

'Nonsense. You had nothing whatever to do with it. If anyone's to blame, it's me. Now then …' Purbright looked about him – 'I suppose we'd better view the remains. Where'd you put them?'

'I didn't put them anywhere. They're … he's just sitting there in the lounge.'

Purbright took the key Love offered. He paused. 'By the way, where's the girl?'

'She's up in their room.'

'Upset?'

Love looked uncertain. 'Well, shocked of course; she was there when it happened. But not hysterical or anything.'

Purbright beckoned the others. He unlocked the door.

On the far side of the long room, with its indigo ceiling, pearl-grey walls and scallop-backed armchairs panelled with alternate plum and yellow, sat a solitary figure. It seemed to have been waiting for them there a long, long time. Slumped a little sideways in the big, embracing chair, it stared stupidly as if just awakened from a doze.

In front of the chair was a low, kidney-shaped table bearing a tray set with a teapot, milk, sugar, and two cups and saucers. One eye of the corpse seemed directed at the pot; the other fixed upon the advancing party, defying them to ask for a share in the refreshment.

The police surgeon bent over the body, lightly touched eyelids, wrist and neck, and stood back. With a pencil he pointed to a spot just above the dead man's collar, an inch or so to the left of his windpipe. 'There's the puncture,' he said to Purbright. 'That little bluish mark.' They all drew close and peered, heads together, at the throat of the dead Mr Periam.

Purbright made a rapid survey of the table top. 'Where's the lighter, sergeant?'

'On the floor, sir. There, by his left foot.'

Very cautiously, Purbright picked it up and held it in his open palm. 'You'd better tell us just what happened. From the beginning.'

Love gave a frown of concentration. 'Well, I'd taken the thing round to everyone I could think of who knew Mr Hopjoy – George Tozer first, then one or two of the people in Beatrice Avenue. They didn't recognise it, so I tried a few licensees in town. I hadn't much luck with them, either. Then I thought that Mr Periam would be the best bet, even though it meant coming right out here. Well, they'd lived in the same house, after all. He recognised it at once. "That's old Brian's," he said. "Where did you get hold of it?"'

'They were sitting here, were they – Mr and Mrs Periam?'

'That's right, sir. The girl at the desk told me to come through. They were quite friendly. Asked me to sit down – I sat in that chair over there – and I took the thing out of the envelope. I hadn't let any of the other people actually handle it – well, I understood it was evidence, in a way – but Mr Periam leaned across and took it before I could stop him. He said, "Oh, yes, I've seen this lots of times," and started to try to get it to light – you know, as anyone might out of curiosity. He kept on pressing the top. It didn't even spark, though. Then he spotted that little trigger thing on the side and pushed it with his thumb nail. There was a sort of hiss – very sudden, with a bit of a pop about it – and he dropped the lighter and felt the front of his neck as if he'd been stung. He said, "That's a queer do" – oh, three or four times; he kept on saying it and rubbing his neck. Then after a bit he couldn't seem to get his breath and just sat there staring and choking. Mrs Periam ran out for help while I held him. But within a minute or two he'd had it.'

Purbright turned to Ross. Gingerly, but knowledgeably, Ross took the lighter between thumb and forefinger and examined it. 'Very neat. Czechoslovakian, probably. I need hardly say that our people aren't issued with quite this sort of thing.'

'Naturally not. How did Hopjoy get hold of it, though?'

'Won it from one of their people's baggage, perhaps. Or he could have bought it. As a souvenir, you know. Some of their chaps are hopelessly mercenary.' He dismissed the point with a shrug. 'See that little hole? The thing's a sort of airgun, really. Primed with the plunger and set off with this catch. Tiny cyanide pellets, I expect. That's the usual drill.'

Pumphrey heard the exposition with marked disapproval. He put his hand on Purbright's sleeve. 'You'll see that this contrivance doesn't get bandied around, won't you, inspector? It would be most undesirable, security-wise, if …' He broke off, looking worried.

Purbright appeared not to have been listening. He gazed thoughtfully at the dead man's face. It looked puffy, stupid, impotent. Purbright felt constrained, as he often did, to attempt the loan of some little dignity to one who had lost all his own. 'You know,' he said quietly to Ross, 'he would have done awfully well in your line.'

'He'd have needed a course in booby-traps first.'

'No doubt. But that' – Purbright weighed the lighter in his hand – 'was just bad luck. Booby-traps, in a much more subtle sense, were his forte. The criminal who proves too clever is common enough; but I must say I'm enormously impressed with a criminal who is able to calculate exactly to what degree the police will prove too clever, and who arranges his crime accordingly.'

Two ambulance men and a constable had entered and were standing hesitantly near the door. Purbright motioned them over. Like tactful, proficient club stewards called to remove a member regrettably immobilised by port, they advanced noiselessly upon the corpse, tweaking up their sleeves. The doctor nodded and departed.

The others moved to a table farther away. Over his shoulder, Love stole a last glance at Periam before a sheet rendered him mere freight.

'It's funny,' he said, 'but he doesn't look the type to smash a bloke's head in with a hammer.'

'He didn't,' said Purbright. 'I think we'll find that strangling was the method, actually. Warlock should enjoy himself looking for skin fragments on Periam's chest expander. "Doing his exercises" was how Miss Cork put it. Now we can add it to our collection of wisdom after the event.'

'You mustn't be too hard on yourself, Purbright.' Ross delicately scraped a few flakes of carbon from the bowl of his pipe with a reamer fashioned (as he could have disclosed) from a secret Skoda steel tool and capable, when keyed to the spindle of an ordinary electric shaver, of grating armourplate away like cheese.

'I'll try not to be,' Purbright said humbly.

Ross looked up. 'There's one question that hasn't been answered. And it's so important that I'm going to put it frankly to you here and now. For whom was Periam working?'

There was a long pause. Then Purbright sighed. 'I'm afraid, Major Ross,' he said, 'that this is where we must acknowledge that we inhabit quite different worlds. You see, the only answer I can honestly give to that question will be meaningless in the context of your work and your interpretation of this case. You will consider it fatuous, if not completely idiotic. Perhaps we should leave it at that.'

'Not at all. I'm interested in your opinion. I really am.'

'All right, then. I believe that in so far as Periam was working for anybody – and I shouldn't have used that phrasing myself – it was for his mother.'

'Ah, Freud comes to Flaxborough!' Ross's broad smile was caught by one of Pumphrey's nervous, sidelong glances of inquiry, and promptly emulated; unfortunately, mirth sat upon Pumphrey's countenance as gracefully as a drunk on a catafalque.

Purbright looked mildly surprised. 'Oh, yes; even in Flaxborough we have our compulsions, you know. Periam's, I fancy, was partly a natural desire to avenge himself on his young lady's seducer – you'll notice, by the way, how carefully he hid this motive by pretending that she was Hopjoy's girl – but what really pushed him to murder could have been the knowledge provided by the Cork woman, and possibly confirmed by his own observation afterwards, that it was that shrine of a bedroom that had been desecrated.'

'In that case,' said Ross, 'why didn't he kill the girl as well?'

'We can't say for certain. Perhaps he had something in store for her later – two murders at the same time would have been infinitely more difficult to conceal than one, and Periam had a strong self-preservative instinct. Or he may have considered that making her a party to the crime was a more fitting punishment.'

'You think she was in it, do you, sir?' Love asked eagerly.

'I think she believed Hopjoy was being got rid of, in the sense of being frightened out of the town – I put it no higher than that. She couldn't have been averse to the idea; her affair with the fellow had been merely a bit of secretive self-indulgence to relieve the tedium of an unconsionably long engagement. As soon as Periam produced the special licence, Hopjoy was out. It was she, of course, who made that phone call, the one described so convincingly by Periam – and remembered by the night porter here, incidentally – which was supposed to have conveyed Hopjoy's summons to a showdown at Beatrice Avenue. She may or may not tell us what she thought the object of it was, but it certainly made her an accomplice, if only technically.'

Pumphrey, who had been tugging his ear-lobes even more ferociously than usual, now impatiently tapped the table with one finger. 'It seems that what you are trying to argue, inspector, is that Hopjoy was liquidated' – 'Literally,' murmured Purbright, but the interjection was ignored

– 'for reasons quite unconnected with his work, his special work, I mean – I think you understand.' Pumphrey threw poor Love a quick glance of distrust, then glared challengingly at Purbright. 'To be frank, I simply cannot understand how an experienced police officer could be so naïve.'

Ross shifted uncomfortably in his chair. 'Oh, come now, Harry ...'

Purbright raised his hand. He regarded Pumphrey genially for several moments. Then he said: 'Thimble Bay ... that's what you're worried about, isn't it. Mr Pumphrey? Right. Well, do you know the nature of the establishment at Thimble Bay?'

Pumphrey's slightly open mouth snapped shut. He looked as if he wished to stopper his ears against impending blasphemy.

'I hadn't meant to tell you this,' Purbright went on gently, 'but I feel it's only fair to ... to put you in the picture fact-wise. About a month ago, a poacher friend of mine left England to live with a daughter in Tasmania. He told me he'd spent quite a lot of his time at Thimble Bay. All that perimeter wire has created a rather nice little wild-life sanctuary. And as long as he was careful not to trip over the remains of two old army huts and to avoid falling into a great overgrown pit, he could take all the hares and pheasants he'd a mind to.' He paused lightly. 'You see, the place was abandoned for some reason or other nearly eight years ago. I feel sure there must be a mention of the fact somewhere in your people's archives, even if Hopjoy seems to have been unaware of it.

'The point, Mr Pumphrey is this. We all have a streak of naïveté in us. It is only when that natural simplicity is allied to an obsession of some kind that all power of

186

discrimination seems to be lost. That is why the credulity of some clever men is so monumental.

'Hopjoy was a fraud. I think even you must see that now. He traded on credulity – and not least on the credulity of his own employers. What got the poor fellow into trouble finally was not his false pretences but his determination to seize every opportunity of ... what shall I say? ... of brushing up his carnal knowledge.

'He underestimated Periam, if indeed he thought of so dull a dog at all, and never guessed, of course, that the fantasy life he had created for his own purposes was a gift to the man who was going to murder him. Hopjoy's end was a classic case of being hoist on one's own petard, and Periam planned it brilliantly and precisely as such. He knew that the more thorough the ensuing investigation, the more compelling would be the evidence of Hopjoy's having engineered his own disappearance.

'Consider that pork we were meant to suppose the clever Hopjoy had purloined for his acid bath. Not just anybody's pork, of course – but half a pig stolen from the Croll's farm, one of Hopjoy's known haunts. It's only now we know the rest of the story that we can see the significance of Periam the tobacconist having been on chatting terms with Hicks the butcher and slaughterman in the shop next door.'

Purbright paused to look down the room at where the heads of some of Mr Barraclough's non-residents could be seen through the glass of the door. They peered in, pushed and conferred. One or two stared resentfully at the privileged occupants, then made off with manager-seeking expressions.

'Tell me, Major Ross,' Purbright resumed, 'did you ever actually see this man Hopjoy?'

'Not as far as I know. Of course, names don't necessarily signify in our game.'

'Quite. No, I was just wondering about his physique. The point is one that I've been unforgiveably slow to appreciate. Heaving ten-gallon carboys and sides of pork is not an exercise for the puny. Periam saw his danger there; he carefully provided a picture of his victim as a fit, husky fellow. One of his most risky lies was the pretence that Hopjoy had emerged unweakened from hospital. I'm sorry to have to say that our old and mutual friend, security, helped Periam there, too. But that doesn't absolve me from having forgotten all about certain trophies of Periam's on his sideboard. They were for weight-lifting ...'

'Ah, well ...' The inspector rose and stretched. 'We mustn't reproach ourselves, gentlemen. Things have really cancelled themselves out rather neatly after all. If they've proved anything, it's simply that time wounds all heels' – his eyes flicked slyly to Pumphrey – 'as Marx so succinctly put it.'

Pumphrey gaped, as if with sudden gastric seizure.

The inspector patted his arm kindly. 'Oh, not Karl,' he said. 'Groucho.'

Preview

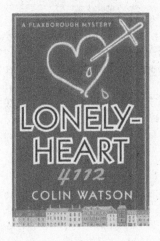

Whatever can have happened to Lil?

Flaxborough butcher Arthur Spain is worried that his sister-in-law hasn't been in touch lately, so he pays her a visit. But Lil's not at home, and by her porch door are a dozen bottles of curdling milk… Alarmed, he calls in the local police, D.I. Purbright and his ever-reliable Sergeant Sid Love.

It transpires Lilian Bannister is the second middle-aged woman in the town to mysteriously vanish, and the link is traced to a local lonely hearts agency called Handclasp House. So when a vulnerable-seeming lady with the charming title of Lucy Teatime signs up for a romantic rendezvous, the two detectives try extra hard to look out for her. But Miss Teatime has a few surprises of her own up her dainty sleeve!

A Flaxborough Mystery, Book 4

OUT NOW!

About the Flaxborough Series

What strange passions seethe beneath the prosperous surface of Flaxborough town? Affable but diligent Detective Inspector Purbright is tasked with uncovering the underbelly of greed, corruption and crime. A classic British series of police mysteries, laced with wry humour.

The full series –

Coffin, Scarcely Used

Bump in the Night

Hopjoy Was Here

Lonelyheart 4122

Charity Ends at Home

The Flaxborough Crab

Broomsticks over Flaxborough

The Naked Nuns

One Man's Meat

Blue Murder

Plaster Sinners

Whatever's Been Going on at Mumblesby?

About the Author

Colin Watson was born in 1920 in Croydon in south London.

At age 17 he was appointed cub reporter on the Boston Guardian, a regional newspaper. His years as a journalist in the Lincolnshire market town proved formative, and he collected there much of the material that provided the basis for the Flaxborough novels.

He won two CWA Silver Dagger awards, and the Flaxborough series was adapted for television by the BBC under the title Murder Most English. Watson died in 1983.

Note from the Publisher

To receive background material and updates on next releases in the Flaxborough series, sign up at farragobooks.com/flaxborough-signup